SAFE AT LAST

To Lord Kirkly's surprise, he saw the colour rise in Otila's pale cheeks as she said:

"I was thinking of a somewhat different disguise..."

"What is that?"

There was a pause before she said in a low voice a little hesitatingly:

"That...I should travel as...your wife!"

Lord Kirkly stared at her.

"You must see it is the only possible solution."

The way she spoke made Lord Kirkly think that this seemed not unreasonable.

And yet he knew that if Otila's disguise was penetrated, it would cause an even greater scandal than anything he had been involved in before.

He rose to his feet, saying as he did so:

"It is impossible! An impossible idea and one I would not entertain for a moment!"

A Camfield Novel of Love
by Barbara Cartland

"*Barbara Cartland's novels are all distinguished by their intelligence, good sense, and good nature...*"
—ROMANTIC TIMES

"*...who could give better advice...than the world's most famous romance novelist, Barbara Cartland?*"
—THE STAR

Camfield Place,
Hatfield
Hertfordshire,
England

Dearest Reader,

Camfield Novels of Love mark a very exciting era of my books with Jove. They have already published nearly two hundred of my titles since they became my first publisher in America, and now all my original paperback romances in the future will be published exclusively by them.

As you already know, Camfield Place in Hertfordshire is my home, which originally existed in 1275, but was rebuilt in 1867 by the grandfather of Beatrix Potter.

It was here in this lovely house, with the best view in the county, that she wrote *The Tale of Peter Rabbit*. Mr. McGregor's garden is exactly as she described it. The door in the wall that the fat little rabbit could not squeeze underneath and the goldfish pool where the white cat sat twitching its tail are still there.

I had Camfield Place blessed when I came here in 1950 and was so happy with my husband until he died, and now with my children and grandchildren, that I know the atmosphere is filled with love and we have all been very lucky.

It is easy here to write of love and I know you will enjoy the Camfield Novels of Love. Their plots are definitely exciting and the covers very romantic. They come to you, like all my books, with love.

Bless you,

CAMFIELD NOVELS OF LOVE
by *Barbara Cartland*

Other books by *Barbara Cartland*

A NEW CAMFIELD NOVEL OF LOVE BY

BARBARA CARTLAND

Safe at Last

J®

A JOVE BOOK

SAFE AT LAST

A Jove Book/published by arrangement with
the author

PRINTING HISTORY
Jove edition/March 1986

ISBN: 0-515-08493-X

Jove books are published by The Berkley Publishing Group,
200 Madison Avenue, New York, N.Y. 10016.
The words "A JOVE BOOK" and the "J" with sunburst
are trademarks belonging to Jove Publications, Inc.

PRINTED IN THE UNITED STATES OF AMERICA

Author's Note

FENCING is one of the Arts with a fascinating history going back to the traditions of chivalry. Swords existed since the very beginning of civilisation and the basic movements of fencing have been used by generations of swordsmen.

The foil has been used since the seventeenth century, but fencing has become a modern athletic sport. In Great Britain a renewal of interest began in the middle of the nineteenth century and the Amateur Fencing Association was founded in 1902.

Passports at the end of the last century were printed in copper plate writing and the name of the individual was written in by hand. As there was a large space left for this, it was quite easy for Lord Kirkly to add a wife to his own particulars. The passport which was surmounted by the Royal Coat of Arms was then signed personally by the Foreign Secretary, in this case, the Marquess of Salisbury.

Safe at Last

chapter one

1891

"This will do."

"I hope you will be comfortable, Milord, and if there is anything you require, please ask for it."

The Receptionist bowed politely, and when Lord Kirkly did not answer moved quietly from the Sitting-Room of the Suite, closing the door behind him.

Alone, Lord Kirkly walked across the room to stand staring out of the window, not seeing the sunshine on the tall grey houses of Paris, or the chestnut trees coming into bloom, but thinking with a dark fury of how badly he had been deceived.

When he thought of how much he had spent on Lissette Forche, he felt like striking himself for his stupidity.

An extremely generous man, and he could afford to be, at the same time Lord Kirkly expected value for money and fidelity from his mistress.

He had swept Lissette Forche away from her other admirers, installed her in an extremely expensive and attractive house near the Champs-Élysées, and bought her diamonds that were the envy of every Courtesan in Paris.

In addition to this, he had actually become extremely attached to her because she was so feminine, so appealing, and very experienced when beguiling and amusing the man who was keeping her.

It was always understood that when one of the famous, astronomically expensive Courtesans of Paris was under the protection of a man who paid all her bills and adorned her with jewels, she was faithful to him for as long as the liaison lasted.

It was one of the recognised rules of the game, and it had never struck Lord Kirkly that there was any likelihood of Lissette being the exception.

He had, however, been obliged to leave Paris temporarily and return to England for a three-day visit, partly in order to attend to various matters concerning his estate in Buckinghamshire, but also to have an audience with Her Majesty, who wished him to accept a position at Court.

It was something he would have preferred to avoid, but he found it impossible to refuse the awesome Queen Victoria, who frightened everybody, including her own son.

But she had always had a *penchant* for handsome men, which made her more affable than she usually was on such occasions.

Indeed, when she rebuked him, as he had foreseen she would, for his past behaviour, which had caused a great deal of comment, she did so more kindly and, incredible though it seemed, more sympathetically than Lord Kirkly or anyone else might have expected.

It was inevitable, since he had caused a great deal of gossip if not a scandal in social circles, that his behaviour should have reached the Queen's ears.

"She knows everything!" one of her Prime Ministers once said, and it certainly seemed to be true.

"We are really very angry with you, Lord Kirkly," she had said in what strangely enough was still a girlish voice.

It was ominous that she was using the Royal "we," but her tone was not so censorious as he had expected.

When he replied:

"I hope not, Ma'am," and smiled at her beguilingly, it was obvious that Her Majesty was weakening.

"I hope in future you will take up the hereditary duties which your father and your grandfather performed, and we shall hear no more of such escapades that, to say the least of it, are reprehensible in a man of your position and age."

Because there was nothing he could say to this, Lord Kirkly merely bowed his head, and after a perceptible pause, in which he knew he was supposed to repent his sins, the Queen went on to speak of other matters.

It was, however, a great relief to know that when he left the Palace he was free to return to Paris and to Lissette.

It was his own fault that he had got into so much trouble for enjoying a very fiery *affaire de coeur* in

London rather than on the Continent a few months before, prompting his self-exile.

It was also unfortunate that the lady in question was the exceedingly attractive wife of the Italian Ambassador, who had announced his grievances and his jealousy of Lord Kirkly to all and sundry.

"In future," Lord Kirkly told himself, "I will confine myself to women without husbands and will certainly avoid foreigners who talk too much. I will also if possible enjoy them in a City which caters for such delights, which London has never been able to do properly."

He doubted, however, when he was forced to spend the greater part of his time in England, that he would be able always to observe such a convenient and prudent set of rules.

But for the moment, at any rate, his interest was entirely centred on Lissette, whom he found even more fascinating than the dark-eyed Italian who had roused him to the point where he had become careless.

At least, he thought with satisfaction as the train carried him back to Paris a day earlier than he expected, Lissette did not have a husband and he would not be facing the threat of an illicit duel taking place at dawn, or, in the case of the Italian Ambassador, an international incident.

He was so delighted to be returning to Paris that he decided he would take Lissette to the Rue de la Paix as soon as she was dressed, and buy her a necklace which he knew she had coveted and which they had seen the previous week in the window of Cartier's.

She would thank him in her own wonderful fashion, and he would be amply repaid for what he had expended on her by the sensations of desire that she would arouse in him.

Of all the Courtesans he might have chosen, he knew that Lissette was outstanding and without peer in her own class.

She was French, but since her family originally came from Normandy she had the fair hair and blue eyes that were characteristic of that part of France.

She had also more self-control and was therefore more subtly exciting than many of her rivals.

Lord Kirkly looked forward to a long liaison with her which would delight them both and to which there was no forseeable end.

He even thought that he might persuade her to come to London when he was forced to return to his own country, and was considering finding her a house in St. John's Wood or in Chelsea, which would be as pleasant as, if not superior to, the house he had taken for her in Paris.

The Express which connected with the cross-Channel Steamer got him into the Gare du Nord at the uncomfortable hour of six-thirty in the morning.

Lord Kirkly having been helped into his clothes by his valet looked forward to a bath as soon as he arrived, after which there would be no hurry to dress again until very much later in the morning.

As he drove through the streets that were comparatively empty, he was thinking of how surprised Lissette would be to see him and how beautiful she would look in the morning light.

Because her skin was fair even without the powder,

5

the rouge, and the lip-salve which were the tools of her trade, she still had the bloom of youth that was very attractive.

He always found it rather appealing after the more exotic ecstasies of their love-making.

The carriage drew up outside the small house ornamented at the front with bushes of lilac and syringa that were just coming into bloom.

The front door was open because, as Lord Kirkly could see, one of the servants had been scrubbing the doorstep, but had obviously been disturbed.

Avoiding a pail of soapy water, he stepped into the Hall, threw down his travelling-cape and hat, and walked quickly up the narrow staircase.

Lissette's bedroom faced onto a small garden at the back of the house which was quiet, and the window received the first rays of the sun.

There was a smile on Lord Kirkly's rather hard lips as he planned to wake her with a kiss, then hear her cry of delight because he was back sooner than she had expected.

But as he put out his hand towards the door, before he could touch the handle he heard a voice inside the room speaking French.

To his astonishment, it was a man's voice, and as he stood transfixed and unable to move, he heard Lissette say:

"Must you go, Pierre? I cannot bear you to leave me!"

"I know," a man replied, "but if I linger any longer, I shall be late on parade and be heavily reprimanded by my Colonel."

6

There was a little pause, and Lord Kirkly thought the two people inside the room were kissing each other before Lissette said:

"We still have tonight. You will come to me for dinner?"

"Of course! You know that I will be with you as soon as it is possible to get away, and I shall be counting the hours until I can hold you once again like this."

They were obviously kissing again, and now, as if Lord Kirkly suddenly came back to life, he was aware not only of what was happening, but who was the intruder in his bed making love to his mistress.

Just for a moment he contemplated throwing open the door and denouncing Lissette for her infidelity and using physical violence on her lover.

Then a very English side of his nature, which disliked scenes and dramas of any sort and felt that to show jealousy was beneath his condescension, made him hesitate.

Swiftly he turned back the way he had come, went down the stairs and out through the front door to where to his relief the vehicle which had brought him from the station had not yet driven away.

In fact, his valet, who had sat on the box with the coachman, was just setting the last of his luggage down on the step.

"Put that back," Lord Kirkly commanded, "and quickly!"

Bates, his valet, who had been with him for many years, gave him one startled glance, then obeyed without comment.

The two heavy leather cases which Lord Kirkly had taken with him to London were back in a matter of seconds.

Stepping into the carriage, he said:

"Drive to the Hotel Meurice!"

The horses moved away, and as they did so he realised that nobody had seen him arrive and nobody had seen him leave. So he was in a position in which he could decide what to do at his leisure.

At the same time, he felt humiliated and degraded not so much because Lissette had been unfaithful to him and the unwritten code of honour which governed such liaisons, but because another man, and he knew who it was, should have consumed his food and drink, make use of his house and his mistress, and inevitably felt as he did so that he had scored over him.

Lord Kirkly was not so foolish as not to realise that a great number of men were not only envious of him, but also resented his having so much and being in many ways, even if they would not admit it, their superior.

It was not only that he was rich——a great number of men had money——but also that he was so successful in everything he undertook.

His horses, which he raced both in England and in France, invariably won. He was noted as an amateur pugilist and was considered the unofficial Fencing Champion of both countries.

That he refused to contend in competitions merely enhanced the aura around him and increased the praise that he received from elder sportsmen who deprecated the behaviour of the young when they invited publicity over their achievements.

There was, in fact, practically no field in the world of sport in which Lord Kirkly had not excelled ever since he left Eton.

He was an amateur rider who was known to have ridden over the Grand National course several times without a fall, though his horses ran in the race with professional jockeys on their backs.

He had his own pack of hounds, and it was considered a great privilege to be allowed to be a member of the Hunt, just as invitations to stay at Kirkly Castle were treasured.

It was even whispered that the Prince of Wales had solicited Lord Kirkly for an invitation.

At the age of thirty-three he had made himself an outstanding personality in England in that he was cheered on every race-course, and if he drove down Piccadilly, almost every man, whether he knew him or not, would take off his hat in homage to him.

As far as women were concerned, he had become a kind of ideal, a symbol of everything a man should be.

It was not only because he was so handsome, it was also because he was so dashing, a Rake who should properly have lived in the time of Charles II, and a lover to whom any woman, once he had possessed her, lost her heart irrevocably.

Lord Kirkly was well aware of this, so that it seemed incredible to him that out of all the women he had known and who admired him little short of adoration, he had been made a fool of by a French *coquette* and her military admirer.

Coming on top of the trouble there had been months ago over the Ambassador's wife, it made him feel a sudden fury against the opposite sex that he had never felt before in the whole of his life.

It was as if Lissette had insulted his manhood and made him feel that she had toppled him from the pedestal on which other women had placed him and which he had in fact found extremely enjoyable.

"Dammit! How dare she?" he asked himself.

Then to his own astonishment he began to wonder if the blame lay not with Lissette but with himself.

Where had he failed? How could she of all the women who had fawned upon him and declared their love be immune to his attractions?

'I must be getting old,' he thought, 'and the best thing I can do is to devote myself to sport of a different sort.'

It flashed through his mind that he might go Big Game Hunting. Then he laughed because it was such an obvious solution, and a traditional one at that, to any amorous problem that got out of hand.

It was the well-worn way of escape for a husband who could not bear to face the fact that his marriage was in shreds, or the lover who was turned down at the last minute and was trying to find some way to salve his pride.

"It might be more original to climb some inaccessible mountain in the Himalayas," Lord Kirkly thought.

At that moment the door of his Sitting-Room opened and Bates announced:

"Your bath's ready, M'Lord!"

"That is what I want," Lord Kirkly said.

"I'll order breakfast, M'Lord."

Lord Kirkly did not reply.

He only walked from the Sitting-Room into the equally large and impressive bedroom, in which a bath had already been prepared with extra brass cans of hot water standing beside it.

He was well aware that no Hotel in Paris provided separate bathrooms in a Suite. Instead, there was a whole army of servants to serve hip baths right into the bedroom.

They had muscles bulging in their arms from carrying cans of hot and cold water up the stairs for the guests' baths.

It was in fact the English who were the most troublesome in that respect. They had no idea when they arrived that there was a sigh of resignation amongst the staff, who knew that their arrival meant inevitably that a large number of baths would be required, while the French were content to wash in a basin.

After he had soaked in the hot water for some time and washed away the dirt and the dust of the journey, Lord Kirkly began to feel better.

His valet had laid out on the bed the clothes that they had taken with them to England, and when His Lordship was finally drying himself on a fine Turkish towel, Bates said to him a little nervously:

"Shall I fetch some of your clothes, M'Lord?" .

"Fetch them all, Bates!" Lord Kirkly replied. "And you can do so immediately. If you are asked why, give no explanation, and it will of course be realised when you appear that I am also in Paris."

There was a knowing look in the valet's eyes, but he merely said:

"I'll do as you say, M'Lord."

11

As he spoke there was a knock at the door, and when Bates opened it he saw there was a waiter outside with a tray.

"Take it into the Sitting-Room," he ordered, speaking in quite passable French with a very British accent.

He came back into the bedroom and Lord Kirkly said, pointing to a pile of small change:

"Tip him, then leave and fetch the rest of my clothes."

"Very good, M'Lord."

Finally dressed in his shirt and trousers, Lord Kirkly stood in front of the mirror to arrange his tie round the high, stiff collar that was specially made for him by a shirt-maker in Jermyn Street.

Then as he glanced at the clock and saw how early it still was, he did not put on the tight-fitting morning-coat which Bates had laid out on a chair.

Instead, he slipped on the long silk robe which touched the ground and which he had taken with him to London.

But instead of going into the Sitting-Room he walked again to the window to look out at Paris and feel a sudden distaste for it he had never had before.

Because it was beautiful, it made him think of Lissette's beauty and because it was charming, it also was a part of her.

"I must get away," Lord Kirkly said beneath his breath, "the difficulty is—where?"

He had no intention of returning to London at the moment, knowing that he had no wish to face the curiosity of his friends and be aware when he entered a room there would be a sudden silence because they

12

had been talking about him.

He had come to Paris to let the wind blow the scandal away and the dust to settle and what was far more likely, to replace it with another one.

He had been so certain that all he wanted to do was to stay in Paris, which was always entrancing in the Spring. Then perhaps when things had cooled down a little he would return home.

Now Paris was barred to him as well, and he thought, too, and his lips tightened at the idea, that it would hurt Lissette more than anything else if he did not personally communicate with her, but merely informed her through his Notary that the house was no longer available, and she should move at once.

Every Courtesan expected when her Protector had finished with her to be rewarded appropriately apart from the many gifts she had received during the time they were together.

Lord Kirkly had always been extremely generous with his farewell gifts, knowing that his departure was always painful to the lady concerned.

In most cases this involved a great deal of weeping and wailing.

The fact that Lissette would not be weeping over him except for financial reasons was an added insult, and he told himself that he would not only refuse to give her a single penny but would also make it very clear that she had forfeited even a word of farewell.

He felt bitter, cynical, and furious with himself.

How could he have been so deceived by her protestations of love? How could he have trusted anyone who was obviously untrustworthy, and believed like

13

any callow youth that she had a real affection for him?

"I must be growing senile," he told himself.

Because he could not bear to think of her anymore, he walked across the room and opened the door into the Sitting-Room.

The first thing he saw, to his astonishment, was a large number of cardboard dress-boxes stacked just inside the door.

Then he realised that standing at the window in the same way that he himself had been doing was a woman.

Just beyond her he could see his breakfast-table and coldly, in a voice that seemed somewhat harsh, he said in French:

"You have made a mistake. This is my private Suite."

The woman turned round, and to his surprise he saw that she was very young and very lovely, with large eyes that seemed to fill her small, pointed face.

It flashed through his mind that he had seen her before. Then he was sure he must be mistaken and walked a little farther into the room, saying as he did so, in a slightly more polite tone:

"The management must have misled you and forgotten they had already allocated this Suite to me."

"I knew it was yours, My Lord, and I told them downstairs that you were expecting me."

Lord Kirkly raised his eyebrows.

"Why should you do that?"

"Because I wanted to see you—because I need your help—and when I saw you arrive a little while ago I felt it was Providence that had sent you at exactly the right moment."

14

"I am afraid I have not the slightest idea what you are saying," Lord Kirkly said, "and I think you must be English, so shall we speak in our own language?"

"My name is Otila Ashe," the girl said.

The name seemed to ring a bell, then Lord Kirkly repeated:

"Otila Ashe? You do not mean . . . ?"

She smiled, and it made her look exceedingly lovely.

"Yes, I am the girl with a fortune—the girl the newspapers keep writing about, and will unfortunately soon be busy writing about again."

Lord Kirkly stared at her incredulously.

He had heard about Otila Ashe when nearly two years ago it was learned that the young English girl had been left an immense fortune by her grandfather, whom she had never seen and who was an American.

Her mother, who had died when she was quite young, had married Sir Willoughby Ashe, who shortly after his daughter became an heiress was killed in a hunting accident.

The story seemed to capture the imagination of the Press, and there were pictures of Otila in the magazines and long descriptions of her grandfather's meteoric rise to fame and wealth from railroad investments in the United States of America.

Lately there had not been so much reported about her, and to Lord Kirkly it seemed incredible that she should suddenly appear in his Hotel room.

"I find what you are saying rather bewildering, Miss Ashe," he said. "Before you explain further, perhaps you would sit down and doubtless you would like some breakfast. As I have only just returned to

15

Paris from England, I admit to feeling the need of a cup of coffee."

"I want nothing, thank you," Otila replied, "except to talk to you."

"Then perhaps you will excuse me if I eat while you talk," Lord Kirkly said, "otherwise my eggs will be entirely ruined."

"Which of course would be a tragedy," she said with what he thought was a touch of sarcasm in her voice.

He did not reply but seated himself at the table while she sat down in an armchair nearby.

He noticed as she did so how elegantly dressed she was, and he would not have been the expert he was on women's clothes if he had not realised, and actually she could well afford it, she obviously patronised the most famous of the French dressmakers.

Her hair was neither fair nor dark, but a mixture between the two, with a touch of red in the curls that seemed to have escaped from beneath her hat, which was plainly trimmed, but nevertheless extremely *chic*.

Lord Kirkly ate a mouthful of egg, which, as he anticipated, was growing cold, and as he poured himself a cup of coffee he said:

"Well, Miss Ashe, I am waiting to hear how I can help you."

"I am only praying you will do so, because I am pleading with you as one British subject to another on foreign soil."

"That certainly sounds very dramatic," Lord Kirkly said with a smile.

"It is," Otila replied, "but I suppose I had better start at the beginning."

"I think that would be wise," Lord Kirkly agreed, "because at the moment I am somewhat bewildered."

He glanced as he spoke at the large array of dress-boxes inside the door and wondered how they came into the room.

Then as he sipped his coffee Otila said:

"After my father was killed I lived with my aunt and uncle, and as I was only eighteen last year they thought that before I became a *débutante* and made my curtsy to the Queen I should improve my French and, of course, my knowledge of a foreign country, by coming to Paris."

Lord Kirkly knew this was quite a usual procedure for Society girls and made no comment as Otila went on.

"I think now that my uncle had been approached by the *Comte* de Chalon, who has a daughter of my age and three sons."

There was a note in Otila's voice as she said the last words, which made Lord Kirkly look at her sharply.

As if he had asked the question, she said:

"You are quite right, it is the three sons who are the difficulty, and the reason why I have to escape not only from them, but from France."

"I do not understand," Lord Kirkly said. "If you wish to get away, surely you have only to write to your uncle and ask him if you can return to England? I should have thought as the Season has just started that this was the right time to do it."

"That is what I thought myself," Otila said, "but the *Comte* has made up his mind that I should marry one of his sons, wanting of course my fortune."

Lord Kirkly smiled before he said:

"Surely there was no difficulty in refusing?"

"That is exactly what I have been doing," Otila replied, "with the result that I am a prisoner—a prisoner whom the Chalons have no intention of losing."

Lord Kirkly put down his cup and said:

"Are you seriously trying to tell me, Miss Ashe, that you cannot get away from this family if you insist upon it?"

"The only possible way is what I am doing now," Otila replied, "in coming to you."

She gave a little sigh before she said:

"The pressure on me to decide which of the sons I shall marry has intensified in the last few months, and it has reached the point where, short of physical violence, there is nothing more the *Comte* can do to me to force me to make up my mind."

"I can hardly believe it!" Lord Kirkly exclaimed. "But surely you have written to your uncle?"

Otila laughed scornfully.

"Of course I have written to him, but do you imagine my letters have been posted? No, they are stopped! I have a suspicion, although I cannot prove it, that my handwriting is being forged by someone in the household who writes to my uncle telling him how happy I am and how I wish to stay on in Paris."

"Is that really true?" Lord Kirkly asked.

"I am telling you the truth because I am desperate!" Otila answered. "I wish I could escape without your aid, but unfortunately I cannot do it alone!"

She spoke so sharply that Lord Kirkly looked at her in surprise, and she went on.

"I know what you are thinking. You think I am

18

making a fuss about nothing, and it might in fact be a good idea for me to marry one of the Chalon sons, who come from an old, respected family and are considered by the French to be extremely well-bred. But I have to tell you that I hate them! I hate all men, and I have decided that if I can ever escape from this money-obsessed family, I will never marry anybody!"

She spoke angrily, and the words seemed to spit from her mouth.

Lord Kirkly could not help it, so he laughed.

"I apologise," he said immediately, "but you sound like a small tiger-cub and so intense that I am sorry for anyone who gets in your way!"

"I am sorry for myself," Otila said, "and I am speaking the truth—I hate men! I have no wish to marry one—ever! All I am asking is for you to help me escape from being forced into a marriage which will make me more of a prisoner than I am at the moment."

She made a gesture with her hand before she said:

"You must realise that if they have control of my fortune, they will never let me go. I shall be shut up in their Château in the country and compelled to have babies whether I like it or not, while they will spend my millions enjoying themselves!"

"I can hardly believe what you are telling me!" Lord Kirkly said again.

"It is true—every word of it!" Otila snapped. "And unless she is half-witted as to want nothing else, it is a dreary, miserable life that respectable Frenchwomen live while their husbands have all the fun, and what is more important, all the freedom!"

19

"It is impossible in any country for a young woman to be free," Lord Kirkly argued.

"Not if she is as rich as I am," Otila replied. "As you are aware, I can buy the services of chaperons and guardians, or anything else that makes me respectable. I do not have to have a man—a husband, ordering me about, telling me what I should or should not do, and making my life a living hell with his protestations of love, which really means he wants another million pounds out of me!"

"One day you will meet somebody who will love you for yourself," Lord Kirkly said, feeling as he spoke that it was a rather banal remark.

"And where am I likely to find one, even if I wanted one, which I do not! Do you imagine they would ever let another man come near me? As I have told you, I am a prisoner, a prisoner in their hands, and this is the first time I have been able to get away from them."

"How did you manage it?" Lord Kirkly enquired.

She gave a little laugh which was very attractive.

"I have been planning it for some time," she said, "because I realised that unless I could get away, sooner or later they would wear me down by some means or another, and I would have to accept one of the sons."

She paused before she said in a low voice:

"Lately I have had the suspicion they were drugging my food and making me so feeble mentally that I would agree to anything they suggested."

"I cannot believe that!" Lord Kirkly exclaimed.

"I am sure it is true. I overheard one or two remarks the *Comtesse* directed to her maid, an old woman who looks like a witch, and I am quite certain is up to every trick. I heard them mention the name of an herb which I know affects the brain, and after that I was certain they put it into a tisan they gave me at night because they said it would help me to sleep."

"What did you do?" Lord Kirkly asked.

"I poured it away when no one was looking, but I knew it was only a question of time before they accelerated their efforts by poisoning all my food so that I was either starved or drugged."

Lord Kirkly felt that he was listening to some extraordinary fantasy which could only exist in a young girl's imagination.

And yet he was aware from the way Otila talked that she was intelligent, and that strangely everything she said sounded convincingly true, even though he had no real wish to believe it.

"You were going to tell me," he said, as she was silent for a moment, "how you got away from them."

"The Chalon family are not very early risers," she said, "the *Comtesse* because she always thinks she is ill and the male members of the household because they are always out late when they are in Paris, attending riotous parties with women who cost them so much money, they need mine to pay for it."

The way she spoke made Lord Kirkly think of Lissette.

Then he thrust the thought from his mind to concentrate on what Otila was saying.

"The only freedom they have allowed me is to draw as much money as I want from the Bank to spend on clothes, or on presents for them. I cannot count how many birthdays, special anniversaries, and so on they have had in the last year. I only know that they intimate exactly what presents they would like me to give them, all of which have been extremely expensive."

Her voice was sharp and sarcastic. Then in a different tone she went on.

"But I have been gradually accumulating enough ready money to pay for any journey I might make, and I intend, if it is possible, as soon as the Banks are open, to draw out thousands of francs to tide me over while I am in France."

"Do you think that is necessary?"

"I think," Otila said quietly, in a very sensible voice, "that the moment they realise I am missing, the Police will be alerted at every Railway Station, so that it will be very difficult for me to leave Paris unless I am disguised."

Lord Kirkly put his hand up to his forehead.

"I find this stranger and stranger," he said, "but go on with how you escaped."

"This morning I rose early and put a number of my new gowns in the boxes you see there and underneath them other things I shall require. I told the woman who is my wardress—and that is the right word for it—to come with me, as I wished to visit the dressmakers early to have some of my gowns altered.

"'I have become so thin,' I said, 'that every one of my gowns needs to be taken in at the waist.'

"'It's too early, *M'mselle*, for going shopping,' she complained.

"'Not as far as I am concerned,' I replied. 'You know if I go later there will be people choosing new gowns, and nobody will wish to attend to the alterations needed on my old ones. So we will go now, and if you do not come with me, I shall go alone!'

"This put her in rather a fix because there was no member of the family she could ask at that early hour of the morning, and it was more than her job was worth to let me out of her sight.

"She was always with me wherever I went, listening to what I was saying, reporting everything I did, and practically what I thought, to the *Comte,* or to the *Comtesse!* But she called a *voiture* and we drove off towards the Rue de la Paix.

"Just as we got there I said:

"'I think you are right after all. We will be too early, and I feel rather thirsty. Let me stop at that Café and have a cup of coffee.'

"She agreed, and telling the *voiture* to wait, we sat down outside the Café. I chose a comfortable seat against some bushes, which made us not too conspicuous from the road. I ordered the coffee and when it came I dropped my handbag on the ground so that some of my money spilled out, and as she bent down to help me pick it up I put into her cup some sleeping-pills that I had systematically stolen from the *Comtesse*'s room over the last week, knowing that she took one every night.

"I had crushed five of the tablets into a powder, and as the woman put my handbag and money back on the table I thanked her and poured some cream into her coffee, stirring it as I did so.

"Then I drank my own, chatting to her and watching her slowly grow sleepier and sleepier as the tablets began to work."

"I should have thought you might have killed her," Lord Kirkly remarked.

"I doubt it," Otila said, "but if she does die, it will be in a good cause! Anyway, after about five minutes her eyelids closed and she gave a deep snore, and I knew she was insensible.

"She was fortunately in an armchair, so she could not fall out of it and I pulled one of the pots of bushes nearer to her so that it was even more difficult for anyone to notice her than it was already. Then I left a large tip on the table, and walking towards a waiter who was hovering in the doorway, I said to him:

"'I will leave this lady to wait here until I return. I shall not be long.'

"I tipped him so that he thanked me profusely. Then I drove away and came here to the Hotel."

"Why did you do that?" Lord Kirkly asked.

"Because I knew it was a Hotel where English people stay when they come to Paris, and I prayed there would be somebody whom I could trust and who would help me. Then I saw you arrive and knew you were exactly the person I was looking for."

"I suppose that is a compliment," Lord Kirkly said. "At the same time, I do not know how I can help you."

"With your reputation for ingenuity and originality," Otila said, "I am sure you can think of at least one way by which I can escape."

chapter two

THERE was silence while Lord Kirkly poured himself more coffee. Then he said:

"I cannot honestly believe that things are as bad as you say they are."

"I am not certain how I can convince you," Otila said, "except that I swear to you on everything I hold holy that I am not exaggerating one word of what I have just told you."

The way she spoke was so sincere and her voice so quiet and calm that she was in fact very convincing.

Lord Kirkly sat back in his chair.

"Perhaps the best thing would be to get in touch with your uncle," he said, "and ask him to come to Paris to fetch you."

Otila was quiet for a moment. Then she said:

"I suspect my uncle would be delighted with the idea of my being married so quickly by accepting one of the Chalon sons. I would then be off his hands. He is in ill health, and I am quite certain that even if he and his wife were prepared to make an effort to bring me out this Season, they are relieved that I have not returned to London and they therefore have no obligation to concern themselves with me."

This seemed quite plausible, and Lord Kirkly also thought, although he did not say so, that he had no wish to return to London himself, and he doubted if what he had to say could be put very convincingly into a letter.

"Do you really believe that the Chalons will alert the Police to look for you?" he asked after a moment.

"I am quite certain they will!" Otila replied. "As they have no intention of losing me, it would be quite easy for them to suggest perhaps that I have lost my memory or incurred an accident. Obviously the Police would be able to enquire at the Hospitals and other likely places better than they could."

Lord Kirkly knew that the Police of Paris were noted for being very shrewd and very ruthless if they wished to apprehend somebody.

He was also aware that they were hand-in-glove with representatives of the newspapers, and nothing of any interest that required the Police's intervention did not immediately find its way into *Le Matin, Le Monde,* and all the other daily newspapers.

Quite suddenly the amusing side of what was happening struck Lord Kirkly, and he laughed.

Otila looked at him in surprise and he said:

"Forgive me, but when you arrived, I was wondering what I should do with myself, having unexpectedly had my plans upset. I was thinking I should either have to go Big Game Hunting, or climb a mountain in the Himalayas!"

Otila laughed too.

"That sounds extremely dramatic, but if that is what you are about to do, please let me come with you."

"That would be impossible!"

"Why?"

"Because I can hardly travel about the world with an attractive young woman without causing a great deal of gossip. As you must be aware, it would not matter if the woman in question was of a different class and with very different interests to yours."

"In other words," Otila said scornfully, "she might be interested in you as a man!"

"Exactly!" Lord Kirkly agreed.

"But from your point of view, what could be better?" Otila asked. "I assure you, My Lord, that I have no wish to marry you, and no desire for you to be interested in me, and from what I know about you from the newspapers and from what I have heard, you are rich enough not to wish to acquire my fortune as well as your own."

Lord Kirkly laughed again.

"That certainly sums it up very neatly!"

"Then if you will take me as your companion or assistant or any other position you like to mention, I would be very grateful."

"You know that is impossible!"

"Then how else can I get out of France?"

"I can hardly imagine that even with me to vouch for you, if they are really looking for Miss Otila Ashe, they will find her in whatever country she happens to be."

There was a little silence, then to Lord Kirkly's surprise he saw the colour rise in Otila's pale cheeks as she said:

"I was thinking of a somewhat different disguise, and one which I am sure the Police would accept."

"What is that?"

There was a pause before she said in a low voice a little hesitatingly:

"That . . . I should travel as . . . your wife!"

Lord Kirkly stared at her.

"You must see it is the only . . . possible solution," Otila said. "You can add me quite easily to your passport without their suspecting it was not done by the Foreign Office, and if I disguise myself slightly, it is unlikely that any French Official will be too nosey about the wife of an English nobleman."

The way she spoke made Lord Kirkly think that this seemed not unreasonable.

And yet he told himself that he was mad to entertain such an idea even for a moment.

He knew that if Otila's disguise were penetrated and it were discovered that he, a well-known Peer and Member of Her Majesty's Household, was deliberately aiding and abetting a young girl who was a minor to escape from her natural guardians while she was in France, it would cause an even greater scandal than anything he had been involved in before.

He rose to his feet, saying as he did so:

"It is impossible! An impossible idea and one I would not entertain for a moment!"

"Then what is the alternative?"

Lord Kirkly walked across the room and as he did so was aware of the pile of dress-boxes just inside the door.

"Who brought these upstairs?" he asked.

"The porter brought them," Otila replied.

"So if the Police make enquiries at the Hotel and he tells them you were carrying a large number of dress-boxes, there will be no disguising the fact that you came to my Suite to see me."

Otila gave a little cry.

"I never thought of that, but the porter was a rather goofy man, and you could say that he brought me to the wrong Suite, but not if the boxes are still here."

"Exactly!" Lord Kirkly agreed. "So the best thing we can do is to get rid of them."

Otila rose from her chair.

"Are you saying ... are you telling me that you are going to help me?" she asked.

"Not in the way you suggested," Lord Kirkly replied, "but I will do my best for you, although God knows I am very likely making the biggest mistake of my life!"

"Thank you, thank you! I have been so terrified that you would refuse and I would not know who else to approach."

"I suppose you could go to the British Embassy? After all, that is what they are there for."

"I thought of that," Otila said, "but then I found

out that the *Comte* and *Comtesse* are great friends of the Ambassador, and I am sure they could persuade him that I was suffering from delusions and he would only send me back to their Château with instructions to be a good girl and not get into mischief another time!"

Lord Kirkly laughed.

He knew the Ambassador and he thought that actually was very likely what he would do.

He would certainly find it extremely hard to believe her fantastic story of being kept prisoner.

He found it hard enough himself, and yet at the same time he was convinced that Otila was speaking the truth.

Part of his success as a man was due to the fact that Lord Kirkly had a way with people.

He never condescended to a man or woman, whatever class they might be.

He listened to what they had to say, and he had learnt from long experience to judge those who were telling the truth or putting on an act.

Using his instinct where Otila was concerned, he was prepared to swear that she was being completely honest and truthful with him and, although her story sounded like something out of a novelette, he knew with what was his sixth sense that she was telling the truth.

He looked at the dress-boxes and saw they all carried the magic name "Frederick Worth," the most famous and most expensive dress-designer in the world.

Then sharply, in a voice of authority that almost made Otila jump, he said:

"Empty the contents of those boxes onto the bed. When my man returns, he will find something in which to pack your things. In the meantime, the boxes must not be seen here in my Sitting-Room."

"I understand," Otila said, "and it is something I should have thought of myself."

She picked up two of the boxes as she spoke and carried them through the door into the Bedroom while Lord Kirkly followed her with the rest.

Quickly they unpacked the exquisite gowns which had been designed by the genius of Worth, who actually as an Englishman.

As she unpacked box after box, laying out not only the gowns but also some exquisite *lingerie* trimmed with lace and embroidered in a way known only to the French who had been trained in the Convents, Lord Kirkly stood once again at the window, looking out into the sunshine and wondering how he could help Otila, while thinking at the same time he was a fool to do so.

He knew he would feel a cad and extremely unsporting if after all he had heard he behaved like a Pharisee and "passed by on the other side."

Every instinct in him revolted at the idea of the Frenchmen, through their greed for her money, goading her to behave in such an outrageous manner.

She was far too young to cope with the world on her own, and he thought she had in fact been extremely ingenious in getting away as she had from a French family of five adults and all their servants, who were determined to keep her in their clutches.

"I will take her out of France," Lord Kirkly decided, "then send her by sea on the first ship I can find back to England."

It was an easy thing to say, but he had the feeling it might be more difficult than it sounded.

"There, I have finished!" Otila's voice said behind him. "And no one coming into the room would know what was hidden on your bed."

Lord Kirkly looked round to see that she had replaced the damask cover which matched the curtains over the bed.

Although it looked slightly rumpled and lumpier than it had before, there was nothing to attract the attention or suggest there was anything unusual about it.

"Good!" he said. "Now I will tie the boxes together as they were when you arrived and try to decide what should be done with them."

"The best thing, I think, would be to put them in another suite on the same floor," Otila said, "and hope that the porter, if he is questioned, thinks that was where he took me when he brought me upstairs."

"I still think they might come up to my Suite," Lord Kirkly said. "The man at the desk will remember that you asked for me."

"What will you say if they question you?" Otila asked.

"I shall say, and my valet will confirm it, that I was having a bath when you called and that you gave him a note for me. Then you left and I did not even set eyes on you."

"I think the Police might believe that!" Otila exclaimed. "But where are we going to put the boxes?"

As she was speaking she and Lord Kirkly were tieing the string round them so that they could all be moved together.

Then he picked them up, noting that they were comparatively light in his hands.

"Open the door," he said, "and see if there is anybody outside in the passage."

Otila obeyed him, peeping out stealthily, then looked back to say:

"It is quite clear!"

"Very well," Lord Kirkly said, "I shall have to risk being seen, and just pray that no nosey chambermaid will appear and think what I am doing is strange."

As he spoke he walked through the door carrying the boxes and hurried down the passage with them to where there was a secondary staircase that was not usually used by the guests.

At the top of it there was a window looking out on the back of the Hotel.

A number of other rooms made a wing which jutted out on one side of it and on the other there was an ugly iron fire-escape which led down to a small courtyard containing a few dusty bushes and several ancient dustbins.

It looked drab and sordid. Carefully Lord Kirkly looked out through the window, saw there was no one about, and pushed the boxes over the ledge.

They floated down into the courtyard, glancing off the top of the bushes and settling behind them so that Lord Kirkly knew they would not be immediately obvious to anyone coming into the courtyard directly from the Hotel.

He did not waste any more time, but closed the window which he had found open and walked swiftly back to the Suite.

Otila was at the door as he reached it and asked anxiously:

"Is it all right? Where have you put them?"

Lord Kirkly told her and she laughed.

"That was clever of you, very clever. If they are found, and there is no reason why it should not be for a long time, they will believe they originally belonged to one of the guests staying at the Hotel."

"That is what I hope they will think," Lord Kirkly said. "At the same time, I think it would be a mistake to stay here just in case you are right and the Police come making investigations as to whether anyone has seen a rather pretty young woman carrying a large amount of dress-boxes."

Otila looked at him wide-eyed. Then she asked:

"Where are we going? And how?"

"That is what we have to decide," Lord Kirkly said. "As to your suggestion that you could disguise yourself—have you any idea how you can do so?"

"What I would really like is a wig," Otila said. "I could dye my hair black, but that would take time."

"Too much time," Lord Kirkly agreed, "and I can assure you anyone who dyes their hair always looks peculiar, especially if they have dyed it black when their skin is fair."

Otila looked at herself in the mirror that was over the mantelpiece.

"The trouble is," she said, "I look so young. How can I make myself look older?"

"Most women would reverse that question!" Lord Kirkly laughed.

"Most women have only to worry about their looks, not about their money!" Otila said. "With the exception of enabling me to buy myself some pretty gowns, my money so far has been nothing but a nuisance. It is a pity my grandfather did not leave it to somebody else!"

"I suppose I should now give you a lecture on ingratitude," Lord Kirkly said, "and point out to you how much good your fortune could do in the world if properly spent."

"I have heard that already," Otila replied, "and I agree, but I do not consider charity extends to the Chalons spending it on riotous living and the type of women they find desirable!"

The way she spoke so scathingly made Lord Kirkly ask:

"May I point out, Miss Ashe, that you are speaking about the sort of woman whom you, as a lady, should not know to exist?"

"I would have to be blind, deaf, and dumb not to do so!" Otila said crossly. "The *Comtesse* is always crying her eyes out because Louis, he is her oldest son, has, according to her, lost his heart and his head to an actress from the *Théâtre des Variétés* who forced him to run up debts which ended in the *Comte* having to sell half of one of his vineyards."

"A very sad state of affairs!" Lord Kirkly said with laughter in his voice. "And what about the other sons?"

"Jules, who his father decided was the most suitable of these three nauseating creatures to be my husband, made no secret when he was at home that he much preferred his *garçonnière*, where he entertained the models who posed for the artists in Montmartre. One in particular, called Mimi, because he had not given her enough money, arrived at the house in Paris and made such a terrible scene that the only way they could rid themselves of her was to pay her off."

"I have never heard of such a thing!" Lord Kirkly exclaimed. "The Chalons must be demented to run their affairs so inefficiently that you as their guest should be aware of what was happening, or that women from Montmartre should dare to call at a respectable house."

"That is exactly what the *Comtesse* says, but nobody listens," Otila replied.

Lord Kirkly was in fact very shocked.

In all his dealings with *coquottes* like Lissette, and there had been quite a number of them, he had never had a scene of the sort that Otila had described, and they never in any way encroached on his ordinary life as a Peer and an English gentleman.

As if Otila knew what he was thinking, she said:

"It all comes down to one thing. The Chalons all live in a manner they cannot afford, and that is why they need my money, and need it desperately!"

"Well, if I can help it, they shall not have it," Lord Kirkly answered. "I have never heard of such disgraceful behaviour, and that you, a young girl who should know nothing of such matters, should have been involved."

"I am sure Papa would have felt exactly the same," Otila answered, "and if he had not died, none of this would have happened."

"Then I can only hope when I get you back to England that your uncle will be more careful to whom he entrusts you another time."

Otila did not say anything, and he had the feeling she was no more eager to return to England than he was, but that was another matter and one he did not intend to discuss with her.

Suddenly they heard the Bedroom door open and Lord Kirkly said in a tone of relief:

"Here is Bates!"

He went to the door between the two rooms and saw Bates coming into the Bedroom carrying a suit-case, and a porter walking behind him with three more.

The man was tipped and when he had left Lord Kirkly said:

"Thank goodness you are back, Bates. Were they surprised to see you?"

As he was speaking he walked into the Bedroom and closed the door so that Otila would not hear what was being said:

"There is ever such a commotion, M'Lord," Bates said with a glint in his eye which told Lord Kirkly he had enjoyed every minute of it. "I goes up to your room to start packing and someone must 'ave told *M'mselle* I was there. 'Er comes rushing in saying:

"'Why are you here? His Lordship—he is back?'

"'His Lordship arrived in Paris early this morning, *M'mselle*,' says I.

"For a minute she was stunned, then she said:

"'Why has he not come here?'

"'He did, *M'mselle*,' I answers, and there wasn't no need for me to say any more!"

"Did she ask you where I was?" Lord Kirkly asked.

"Yes, she did, M'Lord. Pleaded and begged me to tell her."

"But you did not?"

"No, M'Lord. I merely packs your luggage and left the 'ouse."

"Good!" Lord Kirkly said. "And now, Bates, we have another rather different problem to solve."

Because Bates had been with Lord Kirkly for over ten years, and because he trusted him implicitly, he told the man briefly what was happening to Otila and how they had to get her out of France without the Police being aware of it.

He knew as he spoke that Bates was enjoying the drama, just as his valet enjoyed it when he himself was involved in some escapade or another from which he had to be extricated.

"I'll certainly 'elp you, M'Lord," he said. "Has Miss Ashe any suggestions as to 'ow she can get away?"

"Only one, but it is one that I would not entertain," Lord Kirkly said, "and that was that she should travel with me as my wife!"

There was a pause before Bates said:

"That's an excellent idea, M'Lord, if I may say so. No one would dare to insinuate that Your Lordship's wife was anything but what she professed to be. But of course the lady'd have to disguise herself a little."

He knew that Lord Kirkly was looking at him enquiringly and he said:

"I've seen pictures of her, M'Lord, in the newspapers. I remembers the headlines about her fortune and thought what a lucky young lady she was."

"Well, she is not being very lucky, at the moment," Lord Kirkly said, "and that is why we have to help her."

"Of course, M'Lord! I wouldn't expect Your Lordship to do anything else."

There was a note of admiration in Bates's voice that Lord Kirkly did not miss, and he thought ruefully of his sporting reputation and the escapades in which he had often been involved.

He supposed it was inevitable that he would be cast as a Knight Errant in a situation such as this.

"Now, listen, Bates," he said. "I am in enough trouble at the moment as it is. Whatever wild schemes you and Miss Ashe may have for me, they had better be successful, otherwise I shall find myself exiled from England for a very long time!"

"I 'opes not, M'Lord!"

Then in a different tone of voice, as if Bates were getting down to work, he said:

"I s'pose, M'Lord, it wouldn't be possible to find out exactly 'ow this *Comte* is planning to get Miss Ashe back into his clutches?"

Lord Kirkly looked at the man, then he said:

"That is an idea!"

He opened the connecting door and found as he expected that Otila was waiting for him and looking very worried.

"It is all right," he said soothingly. "Bates is here and full of ideas as to how we can help you. It would be useful if we knew what the Chalons will do when they find you have gone."

He looked at the clock as he spoke and said:

"I should imagine by now your sleeping Wardress has been discovered by the people at the Café, and if they realise she has been drugged, will they know who she is?"

"I did not tell you before," Otila said, "because it seemed rather reprehensible of me, but before I left her I opened her handbag. There was nothing in it to prove her identity except for a letter addressed to her care of the *Comte*. I brought that away with me."

Lord Kirkly laughed.

"You have been more resourceful than I could have expected, and very much more intelligent."

"I am fighting desperately for my freedom," Otila said in a low voice.

"Now, tell me something," Lord Kirkly said. "Does the *Comte* have any race-horses?"

"Yes, of course, but they are not very good ones like yours. However, he does occasionally win races at Chantilly, where he came in second a month ago, and at Longchamps."

"Excellent!" Lord Kirkly said. "I am going to write to him suggesting that I have heard he has some horses for sale. Is that a possibility?"

"I am quite certain he would be prepared to sell anything he possesses!" Otila replied. "But he is unlikely to have any worthy to be in your stables."

"That of course I could not know until I have seen them!"

He sat down at the desk in a corner of the Sitting-Room and opening a drawer found, as he expected,

40

some writing-paper headed with the name of the Hotel.

He wrote a note in flowery French, which showed how proficient he was in the language, then handed it to Otila to read.

It was quite brief and simply said that he had just arrived in Paris and had heard that the *Comte* had some horses for sale and would be very interested in seeing them.

Would he be kind enough to suggest a date in the next few days when they could meet?

"I am sending Bates round to the house with this immediately," Lord Kirkly said, "and knowing Bates, I am confident that while he is waiting for an answer he will find out anything else we need to know."

"That is a clever idea. I only hope it is not dangerous for you."

"There is no reason why it should be," Lord Kirkly replied. "By the time we get an answer we will be ready to leave, so I suggest if there is anything you particularly want, that you tell Bates to buy it on the way to the *Comte*'s house. He will also have to purchase an extra case in which to pack your clothes."

Otila smiled at him, which told him better than words how grateful she was.

* * *

Ten minutes later Bates had left with the note and a list of things which he knew he could buy in the nearest shop to where he was going.

"Now all we have to do," Lord Kirkly said when

41

Bates had gone, "is to decide where we will cross the border of France and into which country we should go. Then how from there we shall get back to England."

Once again he was aware that Otila was not at all keen on the idea of their going to England.

At the same time he had no intention of taking her any farther once she was out of danger.

"There is quite a wide choice," he went on, "seeing how many countries have frontiers with France. There is Belgium, which I always think is a dull country, and there is Germany..."

Otila wrinkled her nose and he said with a smile:

"I agree with you! Switzerland is impossible, as there would be no ship from there to carry you back to England. That leaves Italy, which I should think would be our best bet, and Spain."

"I agree Italy would be best," Otila said quietly.

Lord Kirkly, however, was thinking of the flashing eyes of the Ambassador's wife who had got him into trouble in the first place, resulting in his coming to Paris, where he had found Lissette.

He felt because of her that Italy had no particular enchantment for him at the moment.

He wondered if he did go there whether it would be possible for the Ambassador, who had been extremely vindictive, to make more trouble for him than he had already.

Then he told himself there was no reason for His Excellency to be aware that he was in Italy, except of course that with his name and his reputation there were few places in the world where he could be for long and remain anonymous.

"You are worried," Otila said in a quiet voice. "I feel you would rather not go to Italy."

"Why should you think that?" Lord Kirkly asked sharply. "And if you are reading my thoughts, I wish to keep them to myself!"

He sounded so irritated that Otila laughed.

"I am sorry," she said, "but because I have been so on my guard all these months, I tend to listen to every intonation in a person's voice and to notice every expression in his eyes in order to safeguard myself. So now when I watch you I am aware of what you are feeling."

"Very well, I agree that Italy is not ideal, but I cannot think where else would be more appropriate in our desire to leave France unnoticed."

He was quiet for a moment, thinking it out for himself, then he explained:

"In the first place, there will be more tourists at this time of the year going to Italy, and secondly, the Italians are notoriously lazy about checking passports and papers, whereas in Germany we should be scrutinised from our heads to our feet."

"Then please do not let us take any risks," Otila begged. "I am so frightened that something will prevent us from getting even as far as the frontier or that you might . . . change your mind."

"I think, Miss Ashe—no, Otila!—I cannot go on calling you 'Miss Ashe,' especially not when you are supposed to be my wife," Lord Kirkly said. "I am too far committed to back out. Of course, I may find a reasonable excuse for doing so when Bates returns to tell me that no one is worrying in the least about your disappearance, and you are exaggerating their interest in you!"

Lord Kirkly was not speaking seriously and was teasing. But for a moment Otila stared at him incredulously. Then she said:

"How can you be so . . . unkind as to . . . frighten me? I thought for a moment you meant it, and you were going to back out and . . . leave me to . . . my . . . fate."

"And what would you have done then?"

"Perhaps I would have murdered you!" she said. "That would give me a long term in prison, if not the guillotine. To die would be better than having to marry Jules de Chalon!"

Lord Kirkly laughed.

"Now I am certain you are being over-dramatic and over-playing your hand."

"Perhaps if you understood how terrified I have been this last week or two," Otila said, "you would know I am still too frightened to believe that I really have a chance of getting away! When I am safe, I shall be prepared to go down on my knees and thank you for helping me."

The way she spoke was very moving, and because he was embarrassed, Lord Kirkly sat down in a chair and started to tell her of some of the dangerous spots he had been in at one time or another.

He told her too that it was almost by a miracle that he had come out of them more or less unscathed.

Bates came back before they expected him to, and he walked into the Sitting-Room looking extremely

44

smug and pleased with himself.

As he shut the door behind him Lord Kirkly asked impatiently:

"Well? What happened?"

"There was quite a drama, M'Lord! I 'ands Your Lordship's letter which was taken to *Monsieur Le Comte*, who was at breakfast. I gathered from what the servants said that he was gratified by your interest. I was waiting in the hall chatting up the French servants, so to speak, when a *voiture* drives up and a woman is helped out of it who seemed to have difficulty in moving her limbs, and could hardly walk!"

"That must have been my wardress!" Otila exclaimed.

Lord Kirkly looked at the clock on the mantelpiece and saw it was nearly noon.

"Your tablets have lasted about three hours," he said, "they could not have been as strong as you had hoped."

"Strong enough for me to get away," Otila said in a low voice.

"Go on, Bates," Lord Kirkly ordered. "What happened next?"

"Well, as she walked in through the open door, the *Comte* at that moment comes from one of the rooms, where he's been writing a letter in reply to yours. He's just handed it to me and begun to say:

"'Tell your master...' Then he saw the woman who had just arrived.

"'*Madame* Lucien!" he exclaimed. 'What has happened to you?'

"'She's gone—*Monsieur le Comte!*' the woman

45

said in a strange voice, as if it were difficult for her to get her words out.

"'What do you mean—she has gone?' the *Comte* asked.

"'She put a—drug in my—coffee—and when I—woke, it was to find the—waiters trying to—revive me and—saying they must—send for a—doctor.'

"'But *Mademoiselle*—tell me about *Mademoiselle!*' the *Comte* asked, and I can tell you, M'Lord, he was shouting by this time.

"'She's—gone! Oh, *Monsieur*—she's gone!' the old woman said, and slowly collapsed in a heap at his feet!"

"What happened then?" Otila asked excitedly, as if she could not wait to hear.

"You've never 'eard such a commotion, Miss!" Bates replied. "The *Comte* were shouting so loud that an elderly woman who I guessed was his wife came running to ask what was the matter. Then a young man, very smartly dressed, appears from another room.

"'What is it, Papa? What is it?' he kept asking.

"'Otila has escaped!' the *Comtesse* shouted.

"'She will not get far!' the *Comte* added.

"'But you must stop her!' the *Comtesse* insisted.

"'*Oui, Papa,*' the young man said. 'Stop her! If she gets back to England, we will have lost her!'

"'I know that,' the *Comte* replied angrily. '*Mon Dieu!* I could strangle this old fool for letting her slip out of our hands!'

"As he spoke, M'Lord," Bates continued, "I thought for one moment he was going to kick the body of the old woman lying at his feet. Then two servants lifted her up and carried her out of the Hall and by that time the young man had come downstairs.

"'Do something, Papa! Do something!' he shouted.

"They was all screaming and yelling an' throwing their arms about! Your Lordship knows what them Froggies is like when they gets excited!"

"What did they decide to do?" Lord Kirkly asked.

"There's no doubt about that, M'Lord. They all began to scream that someone must send for the Police!"

"'If she is going to England, she will make for the Gare du Nord,' the *Comtesse* said.

"'I am aware of that,' the *Comte* replied. 'But the Police must be on watch at every station just in case she goes south.'

"'I suppose she will have enough money?' the young man said.

"'I heard she cashed a large cheque yesterday to go shopping,' the *Comtesse* faltered."

Bates grinned.

"It was then the *Comte* turned on her and cursed her for not suspecting that Miss Ashe was up to somethin' for which she would need money.

"'It is your fault too,' he went on angrily, 'for putting that old idiot in charge of her. You should have someone young and strong in her place, as I suggested.'"

Bates grinned again and added:

"Then the *Comtesse* began to cry and I thought it was time I left, havin' found out all Your Lordship asked me to do—that they were going to send for the Police."

"You have done very well, Bates!" Lord Kirkly said. "Did you remember to buy a suitcase?"

"It's outside, M'Lord, an' also the things Miss Ashe asked me to get for her."

Lord Kirkly's eyes twinkled.

He was well aware, knowing Bates, that he had wished to make his entrance and the recitation of his discoveries as theatrical as possible.

It would have spoiled the effect if he had come into the room carrying a large case.

Lord Kirkly did not say anything, however, as his valet opened the door and brought in the case which he had left in the corridor. In fact, there were two of them.

As if Lord Kirkly asked the question, he said:

"You won't be able to get all them things on the bed into one case, M'Lord. Besides, it would crush the gowns and they's need pressing."

As it was obvious that Bates assumed he would have to do it, he was saving himself as much work as possible, and once again Lord Kirkly thought the man was incorrigible and at the same time invaluable.

Bates carried the suitcases into the Bedroom and Lord Kirkly turned to Otila.

"There is no time to be lost," he said, "and we must leave for the Gare de Lyon as soon as you are ready."

She gave him a questioning glance and he added ruefully:

"I suppose I have no alternative but to agree that you should travel with me as my wife, and while you are making yourself look the part I will alter my passport."

He paused before he added:

"I presume you know that I am liable to incur a large fine, if not imprisonment, for doing so. But I suppose you could say it is in a good cause."

"All I can say," Otila said in a soft voice, "is that I am very, very grateful!"

chapter three

WHEN Otila came into the Sitting-Room, having been arranging herself in the Bedroom, Lord Kirkly looked up and after a moment's pause laughed aloud.

She had certainly altered her appearance quite considerably from the way she had looked when she arrived in his Suite.

She had pulled back her hair from the sides of her face in a much older style than she had used before, and she had obviously asked Bates to buy her some veiling, which was worn only by older women, and arranged it around her hat.

Besides this, she had on her small nose a pair of ugly spectacles which made her look, Lord Kirkly thought, like a rather intelligent owl.

She watched him appraising her, then she dropped him a mocking curtsy.

"I hope you approve of your wife, My Lord."

"I think it would be difficult for anyone who does not know you very well to recognise you," he said, "which is the only thing that matters."

Instantly Otila was serious.

"I hope you are right," she said. "At least I am sure people who have seen my pictures in the newspapers, as Bates tells me he has, would not know me. But one of the Chalons would certainly be suspicious."

The note of fear was back in her voice, and Lord Kirkly said sharply:

"Then let us hope we do not encounter any of them."

There was a short delay while Bates finished packing Otila's clothes, and those in which Lord Kirkly had travelled from London.

Then they set off for the Gare de Lyon in two *voitures*, Bates and their luggage in one, while they travelled in the other.

When they arrived at the station, Lord Kirkly went immediately to the Station Master's Office, and having announced who he was, made enquiries as to the trains which would carry them into Italy.

He learnt that there was an Express leaving in half an hour, which would go directly to Milan.

The First Class carriages of course could be turned into sleepers, but on enquiry, because the Station Master was impressed by Lord Kirkly and his air of consequence, he managed without a great deal of difficulty to acquire a Drawing-Room carriage, which by a piece of good fortune was already attached to the train, having been used on the journey to Paris from Milan.

When finally they were bowed by the Station Master into their special coach, Otila appreciated that it was prestige as well as money which counted in a mundane world.

She, however, kept very quiet, hoping to remain so unobtrusive that if questioned later, neither the Station Master nor his assistants would remember her.

When at last their luggage was in their coach and Bates was provided with a sleeper in the one adjoining, Otila began to believe that they had got away safely.

Nevertheless, she found it almost hard to breathe naturally until finally the train moved slowly out of the station to a great show of waving flags and blowing whistles.

Then she threw back her veil, pulled off her spectacles, and exclaimed:

"We have done it! At least we are leaving Paris and the Chalon family behind!"

"I sincerely hope so!" Lord Kirkly said. "And I imagine we were ahead of the Police, if there were any, inspecting the passengers at the Station."

There was a little pause before Otila said:

"There were two men who arrived later than we did and I noticed they were scrutinising everybody who went onto the platform. But as we were with the Station Master, they took no notice of us."

Lord Kirkly commended her for her observation, and because he thought it would be a mistake for her to be agitated, he replied:

"At least you have proved your disguise to be effective in one instance, and may I say I much prefer you without those extremely disfiguring spectacles!"

Otila laughed, and it was a very young, spontaneous sound.

"They were certainly easier to put on and take off than a wig, and I also thought that if Bates had bought a wig, it might have been remembered by the people in the shop if there was anything in the newspapers about my having disappeared, and arouse their suspicion."

Lord Kirkly thought a little cynically that she was giving herself undue importance, but still one never knew, and if the newspapers had nothing else very sensational to report, they might certainly write up the story of the missing heiress.

They made themselves comfortable in the Drawing-Room, which was not as large as those to be found on trains in England.

Nor was it anywhere near as big as the one on his private train which he used on special occasions, especially when the race-meetings he attended were a long way from London.

But the French coach was certainly big enough for them, although as Otila discovered a little later with dismay there was only one Bedroom.

She relayed this information to Lord Kirkly, and he smiled.

"Do not look so tragic about it," he said. "Bates will make me up a bed here on the floor, and I could hardly ask for two Bedrooms when we are supposed to be married."

"If anybody sleeps on the floor, it should be me,"

Otila said. "After being so kind to me, I could not bear you to be uncomfortable."

"If you are going to be aggressively bossy," Lord Kirkly said, "and interfere with my arrangements, I shall dump you down on the first wayside station and let you look after yourself!"

"I am not aggressively bossy!" Otila retorted hotly. "I am only thinking of you and your comfort."

"I thought you hated men!"

"I do!" she said firmly. "I loathe and detest them! At the same time, I have to concede that one of them has been very clever in getting me out of Paris, and I am very, very grateful!"

"We must not 'count our chickens before they are hatched,'" Lord Kirkly said. "Now, sit down beside me, Otila, while I tell you what I am planning to do when we reach Italy."

He thought there was a slightly apprehensive look in her eyes, but she obeyed him and sat down in one of the comfortable armchairs.

As she did so he was conscious that she used a perfume that was very fresh and young, and reminded him of spring flowers.

It instantly made him think of the rather heavy scent which Lissette believed was seductive, and which she drenched not only on herself, but also on the pillows of her bed and the sheets.

Now, because he was angry with her, Lord Kirkly thought it was too overpowering and he should not have been beguiled by anything so obvious.

He had not spoken for a minute or two and Otila gave a little cry.

"You are angry!" she said. "What are you thinking about that has made you angry? Is it something I have done?"

Lord Kirkly forced the frown from between his eyes. Then he said:

"No, it is not you, Otila, I was thinking of something else."

"Something that has upset you?"

"I do not wish to talk about it."

"I think that is unfair!"

"What do you mean?"

"You know what I am thinking, and naturally I am curious as to why you seem so . . . disgusted . . . with women."

"Shall I say," Lord Kirkly replied, "that this is a subject which a young girl should not be discussing with a man?"

"Now you are definitely cheating!" Otila said accusingly. "What you are really saying is that I am to mind my own business and not interfere in yours."

"I suppose that puts it very concisely," Lord Kirkly agreed. "So shall we get back to where we started and talk about your future?"

"I suppose I have no choice in the matter."

"None!" he agreed. "What ever you may think of me as a man, I still like to be in command of my own ship, which in this case is a railway carriage."

Otila laughed as if she could not help it. Then she said:

"Very well, I will not tell you how curious I am, but I can imagine far more frightening explanations of your feelings than anything you will tell me."

"I hope they give you satisfaction!" Lord Kirkly said dryly.

"I have been thinking about you," Otila told him, "while we were driving to the station, and I remember hearing from the *Comte* and in the past from my father, how successful your horses have been, and how important you are in Society. That is true, is it not?"

"I suppose so," Lord Kirkly said in a resigned tone. "But I do not see how it affects you at the moment, except to provide us, without difficulty, with this very comfortable railway carriage."

"What I was thinking," Otila said a little mischievously, "was that I was really very clever to find you."

"And now that you have found me, Otila, listen attentively to what I have planned."

He spoke firmly, and as Otila raised her large eyes to his, Lord Kirkly thought they were different from any other woman's eyes he had ever seen.

In sunlight they seemed grey, flecked with gold, but when she was afraid, they turned almost to purple.

He was aware too that everything she felt was mirrored in her eyes, and she was so very lovely that it seemed quite unnecessary for her to have such a large fortune as well.

Then he looked away from her and began:

"When we arrive in Milan, I suggest we do not linger there, which could be a mistake, but proceed immediately either to Genoa or to Naples."

"Why should we do that?" Otila asked.

"Because," Lord Kirkly explained, "that is where my assistance will end, and having placed you on board a ship going directly to England, which should

57

not be difficult to find, I need no longer concern myself with your affairs."

"And where are you going then?" Otila asked.

"You are being inquisitive again," Lord Kirkly replied, "but I will tell you truthfully, that I have not yet made up my mind. I am, however, thinking I might visit Tunis. I have never been there before, and my interest is not only that I have friends in the City, but also that I would like to see the very fine Roman remains that are to be found in the Country."

"I once read a book about them," Otila said, "and Papa had a friend who had travelled all over North Africa and described to me the magnificent temples and other public buildings which the Romans left behind wherever they built towns."

"The alternative," Lord Kirkly said as if he were thinking aloud, "would be to go to Morocco. I have been there before, and I cannot say I am wildly enthusiastic about retracing my steps."

"Then you must go to Tunis," Otila said, "and I wish I could come with you."

Lord Kirkly threw up his hands in an exaggerated gesture of protest.

"No, no! I have made a mistake in telling you what I thought of doing, and it was not an invitation for you to accompany me. I am delighted to have been of service to you, Otila, but now you must stand on your own feet, and I am quite certain that when you are back in England and tell your uncle how badly you have been treated by the Chalons, he will arrange for you to be better chaperoned in future."

"I hope so," Otila replied, "but I have no wish to

be constrained by chaperons and people telling me what I may or may not do. I want to be free! I want to travel and see the world, all the exciting places I have never been to!"

"There is nothing to stop you from doing that, as you can afford to do so," Lord Kirkly said, "but you must choose the right people to go with you, and make quite certain that you do not find yourself in the same predicament as you experienced with the Chalons."

"That is the whole point!" Otila protested. "How can I possibly know what people are like until it is too late? I may meet a charming woman who seems in every way suitable, until I find she has sons or nephews who all have the same idea: to marry me for my money."

"Now I think you are exaggerating the whole thing," Lord Kirkly said firmly. "You are a very pretty young woman and someday a man will undoubtedly love you for yourself and not be in the least interested in your money."

"Do you really believe that?" Otila asked. "But how can I know, how can I be quite sure that any man who says 'I love you!' is not thinking as he does so, how exciting all those millions of pounds are!"

"Now you are being absurdly cynical!" Lord Kirkly exclaimed. "If you are really so frightened of fortune-hunters, perhaps the only thing you can do is to behave, if I have not forgotten my fairy-tales, like the Prince who disguised himself as a beggar so that he would be loved for himself alone."

"That is certainly an idea!" Otila said. "And if I came as your assistant or perhaps your secretary, I might meet a man who would not be interested in anything except me."

"Now you are telling me a fairy-story," Lord Kirkly said, "and let me make it clear once again that I have no intention of taking you with me. We both have to live up to our avowed dislike of the opposite sex."

"I do dislike them!" Otila protested. "I dislike men very much, but I am intelligent enough to realise it is because I have only met them as Miss Otila Ashe, and not as a young girl with no assets except her pretty face."

Lord Kirkly smiled before he said:

"I think that might get you quite a long way, and when you get back to England I should certainly consider it as a possibility. There cannot be so many people who would know you by sight, and as you are so young, you might quite easily set up a new life for yourself as 'Miss Nobody from Nowhere' and see how far you get in the rôle."

"From the way you are speaking," Otila said, "I have the uncomfortable feeling that you would be very surprised if anyone even notices me, let alone proposes marriage."

"I did not say so," Lord Kirkly remarked.

"But it is what you were thinking, and now you have made me apprehensive of trying out what seemed at first to be a very good idea."

"It will give you something to think about on your way home to England."

"Supposing," Otila said in a very small voice, "that the . . . men on the ship are . . . unpleasant?"

Lord Kirkly, as he glanced at her, realised that

the fear was back in her eyes, and he told himself irritably that he really could not be responsible any further for this tiresome child, for she was little more than that.

The idea of trailing around Europe with her was quite impossible, and in any case he did not want a woman with him at the moment.

If there was one, it would be somebody in a very different capacity, in fact, if he was honest, another Lissette.

"Now that is settled!" he said in a slightly over-hearty voice. "We will go to Genoa, and if you are worried about having no one to look after you on the voyage, I am sure there will be some respectable elderly lady amongst the passengers who would be only too glad, for a small fee, to chaperon you very effectively until you reach England."

He felt Otila did not respond very eagerly to this suggestion, but he was determined not to be embroiled any further.

He merely picked up one of the newspapers which Bates had bought at the station before they left and turned over the pages.

After a while, when he still did not speak, Otila rose from the chair in which she was sitting and changed to another one against the window.

She stared out at the passing landscape, and looking at her with her head silhouetted against the sky, Lord Kirkly thought she was in fact very lovely and, however apprehensive she might be, a large number of men would find her very desirable, with or without her fortune.

61

Then he told himself that Otila would always be handicapped by her suspicions of their real motive, and it was inevitable that sooner or later she would become cynical and perhaps bitter, and that would spoil her.

She was intelligent enough to realise that, and he thought actually how very clever she had been in escaping from the Chalons, and acting in a way which few young women in the same situation would have had the courage to do.

There had been, however, a grave risk which he was sure she would not understand, of finding herself embroiled with some Englishman whose behaviour might have been very different from his.

With a faint twist of his lips he wondered what his friends, and certainly his enemies, would say if they knew that at the moment he was travelling with a very lovely, very attractive young girl, officially described as his wife on his passport, who trusted him implicitly, believing him when he suggested he disliked women.

'This is the sort of position in which she should never have found herself,' he thought, 'and I would like to have the chance of telling her uncle so.'

At the same time he had the uncomfortable feeling, when he thought about it, that having put Otila on board a ship at Genoa, he would continue to worry about her simply because she was so young, so helpless, and so attractive.

"It has nothing to do with me!" he tried to tell himself firmly.

But as the hours passed he found it difficult not to

wonder what the future held for Otila and how she would ever cope with it on her own.

Their luncheon which Lord Kirkly had ordered in advance was brought to them when the train stopped at about twelve-thirty, and was certainly improved by the excellent bottle of champagne which Bates bought for them and a pot of the best *pâté de foie gras*.

To Otila it was new and amusing to eat "picnic fashion" in a train, and as they talked over various subjects Lord Kirkly found himself laughing whole-heartedly at things she said and her very astute crit-icisms of the French.

She told him of the many customs of the Chalons, which seemed strange and of course very un-English, and Lord Kirkly felt she had the same keen eye for detail which he had always fancied he had himself.

When they had finished luncheon he said:

"I am wondering when we stop at the next station whether there will be a chance of stretching my legs."

"It would be pleasant to have some fresh air," Otila said.

"It would be a mistake for you to leave the car-riage," he said quickly.

She pouted at him, saying:

"It is unfair that you should have all the fun. I want to walk too, and there might be something nice to buy."

"I very much doubt it," he said, "but I suppose you can come onto the platform if you dress yourself up to look as you did when we were on our way to the train, and do not forget to wear your spectacles."

"It will be a nuisance," Otila said, "but at least it

will help to relieve the monotony!"

"I cannot think you are being very complimentary to me!" Lord Kirkly said. "You should actually be saying that the hours passed by like a flash because we were having such an amusing conversation."

"Is that the sort of thing your 'lady-loves' say to you when you are with them?"

"That is not the sort of question you should ask me," Lord Kirkly replied, "and the word *lady-love* does not come well on a young girl's lips!"

Otila made a face at him.

"I am not a young girl!" she argued. "At the moment I am your 'wife,' and wives have special privileges, I am quite sure, in that they can say whatever they like and it is very difficult for their husbands to stop them."

"I would certainly not allow my wife, if I had one," Lord Kirkly observed, "to discuss anything which I thought was out of place and out of keeping with her position in life!"

Otila laughed mockingly.

"Now I can see how pompous and difficult you would be if you were really my husband," she said, "and I suppose, because you yourself are a roué, you would be far more strict with your poor, wretched wife than any ordinary man would be."

"Who says I am a roué?" Lord Kirkly demanded.

"I am sure I have heard people who talk about your race-horses say you are," she replied. "At the same time, it is very obvious. You were in Paris, you were disgruntled and upset by something, and what in that City could it be but a woman?"

"You are judging me by the Chalons," Lord Kirkly protested.

"Not only by them, but by their friends," Otila said. "Ever since I have been in France I have realised that where Englishmen are interested in horses, Frenchmen are interested in women! In fact, if you ask me, they live, breathe, and dream of girls!"

Lord Kirkly laughed. Then he said:

"I admit there is a certain amount of truth in what you are saying. At the same time, Otila, if you want to be a success as yourself and not as 'Miss Moneybags,' you really must learn to curb your tongue and talk sweetly and gently, as a young girl should!"

"Who made all these ridiculous rules about young girls?" Otila asked. "It must make them extremely boring, and I am surprised that any man should want to marry them! And yet after they are married, it seems they turn into the sophisticated, scintillating, witty women with whom fastidious gentlemen like yourself fall madly in love."

Lord Kirkly laughed again.

"You have certainly thought it out in detail!"

"I have had little else to think about except fending off Louis, Jules, and Jacques de Chalon. The *Comte* made it quite clear that it did not matter which of his sons I married as long as it was one of them!"

She paused before she went on.

"Everyone in the Château knew that he had a mistress in Paris, and she was another extravagance for which my money was urgently needed."

Lord Kirkly thought he might as well give up telling Otila that she should not talk about such things, which were certainly not proper subjects for a *jeune fille*.

At the same time he was astute enough to realise that while she was observant as to what had been going on in the Chalon household, she was in herself very young, innocent, and as far as the world was concerned, ignorant.

It was also a new experience for him to be alone with a woman who made not the slightest effort to entice him as a man.

She merely talked to him as if he were her contemporary, and even teased him, which was something he had not encountered for many years.

"I suppose you enjoy being so important," she said with mischief in her eyes. "It must be delightful to be a man like you, knowing you have only to snap your fingers and every woman will come running. And anything wrong or outrageous you do will be forgiven because you are so rich and handsome."

"If you go on talking like that," Lord Kirkly said, "I shall give you a good spanking, which is something I can see has been most lamentably omitted from your education up to now!"

"Then you will be brought to trial not only for abducting me, but also for assaulting me!" Otila flashed.

"If I were coming to England with you, which I am thankful to say I am not, I should tell your guardian exactly how he should treat you to ensure that in the future you are a credit to the Social World to which you belong."

"I have no wish to be a credit to the Social World,"

Otila replied. "What I really want to be is a man and, if possible, an explorer."

She put her cheek on her hand, and looking at Lord Kirkly with a serious expression on her face, she said:

"Do you think it would be possible, if I disguised myself, that I could travel as a man and do all the things you do without anybody making a fuss about it?"

Lord Kirkly thought with amusement that there had been quite a lot of fuss made about some of the things he had done, but aloud he replied:

"I think you would make a very peculiar-looking man and I doubt if anybody would be deceived by you in such a disguise. Your eyes, if nothing else, would give you away."

As he spoke it struck him that her figure would do the same.

In the exquisitely cut gown she was wearing, made by Worth, her small waist, the curves of her breasts, and the line of her hips were very obvious, and made him think her body must be like that of a Greek goddess.

He was saved from further repartee at that moment because the train began to slow down as they approached another station.

"Now we will be able to go for a walk on the platform," Otila said excitedly.

She hurried into the Bedroom, and Lord Kirkly knew she was putting on the bonnet with the veil and her spectacles so as to disguise herself.

The train was held up for a few minutes before it could draw into the platform, and when Otila came back disguised she stood beside Lord Kirkly as the train moved slowly to where a crowd of passengers and porters were waiting.

The engine was belching out steam and for a moment the crowd ahead of them was almost obscured by it.

Then the train came to a standstill and those who were disembarking hurried from the carriages onto the platform.

A few passengers searched anxiously for seats.

"There is no hurry," Lord Kirkly said, not moving from the window.

But Otila impatiently had already gone to the door at the rear of the coach and was waiting for a porter to open it for her.

Lord Kirkly picked up his hat and followed her.

Then, as she would have stepped down rather gingerly because there was quite a drop to the platform, she gave a sudden stifled scream and turned back into the carriage to collide with him as he was just behind her.

"What is the matter?" he asked.

She quickly turned round towards him so that her back was to the open door.

Then she said in a whisper that was so low he could hardly hear it:

"Jules! Jules de Chalon! I just saw him stepping off the train! He is travelling with us!"

For a moment Lord Kirkly thought it was impossible.

Then the fear in Otila's eyes and in her voice told him that she could not have been mistaken.

Quickly he took charge.

"Go into the Bedroom," he said quietly, "and stay there and do not come out until the train has started off again."

She did not answer but pushed past him and ran like a frightened animal.

Lord Kirkly went to the door of the coach and stood there looking out.

He was waiting for Bates, who he knew would come from the next compartment for instructions.

A moment later the man was beside him.

"Can I do anything for Your Lordship?" he asked.

Lord Kirkly stepped back, and as if he understood without being told, Bates followed him.

"Miss Otila has just seen *Comte* Jules de Chalon stepping out of this train, Bates," he said. "He is travelling with us. Do not let him see you, in case he can identify you, but see if you can recognise him."

Bates went into the Drawing-Room, where there was a window with a curtain which was pulled back on either side of it.

Peeping from behind one so that his face was obscured, Bates scanned the platform, and Lord Kirkly waited, then after a moment Bates said:

"I can see 'im now, M'Lord. He's not the same gentleman as I sees when I went to the house with your letter, but he's very like him."

"Let me look," Lord Kirkly said.

Bates pulled the curtain a little farther across the window and very cautiously Lord Kirkly peeped through the small aperture.

It did not take him long to identify the very smartly but in his opinion, over-dressed young man.

He was standing with his back to the Station, look-ing closely at the passengers who had disembarked from the train, as Lord Kirkly had been going to do, to stretch their legs.

There was an elderly gentleman accompanied by a grey-haired woman, and a number of flashily dressed men who might have been commercial travellers of some sort.

There were a few country folk, easily distinguish-able by their clothes and the fact that they seemed a little lost and nervous in the new world of steam and power.

Lord Kirkly inspected Jules de Chalon carefully and decided that he was prepared to believe everything that Otila had said about him and his family.

Then as the porters began to close the open doors, and those who had been walking about hurried hastily back to their seats, de Chalon returned to his com-partment, which was much farther up the train, and Lord Kirkly, turning to Bates, said:

"We are going to have a problem, Bates, when we reach Milan. How are we to get Miss Ashe out of the Station without her being seen?"

He paused, then added as if to himself:

"Her disguise is good enough to deceive a stranger, but a man who has seen her every day for months and who wants to marry her will recognise her immedi-ately."

"I'm aware of that, M'Lord," Bates said.

"Then what are we to do about it?" Lord Kirkly asked.

As he spoke he was thinking perhaps they would

be wise to leave the train before they reached Italy.

Then he thought that might be even more dangerous.

It was obvious to him that the Chalons had anticipated that Otila might make for Italian soil, and he suspected that one brother would have travelled to Calais, another was here with them, and the third would be helping his father in searching all Paris.

One thing was quite obvious—the Chalons were taking their position very seriously and, what was more, if it was discovered that Otila was with him, he would be in an extremely unpleasant position.

"What the devil are we to do?" he asked again beneath his breath.

It was too late, he told himself, to regret that against his better judgment he had become embroiled in what might be a far-reaching and very unpleasant scandal.

He was so busy thinking about himself that for the moment he had almost forgotten Otila, until he felt her hand on his arm and looked down to find her beside him.

"It was definitely Jules," she said, "and he will recognise me!"

"That is what I was thinking myself," Lord Kirkly said.

"What can I do? Please . . . tell me what I can do!"

"That is what Bates and I were just considering," Lord Kirkly replied. "It is not going to be easy, Otila, but there must be some way by which we can avoid him."

It was then that Bates said with the air of a magician

71

bringing a rabbit out of a hat:

"I've an idea, M'Lord, an' I thinks it's a good 'un!"

chapter four

MUCH to Otila's surprise, she slept peacefully although she had expected to lie awake worrying over the fact that Jules de Chalon was on the same train.

But Bates had been so confident that he could outwit him that she began to believe herself that the little valet was infallible.

He was certainly very competent when it came to arranging that Lord Kirkly spend a peaceful night.

Again Otila tried to persuade him to take the bed and let her sleep on the sofa in the Drawing-Room, but he laughed at her.

"You forget," he said, "that I have been an explorer and have slept in some very uncomfortable places, including a cave which smelled of wolves, which I expected would return at any moment and resent a usurper."

Otila laughed, but she said:

"You have been so kind in helping me, that I do not like to impose on you any further."

As she spoke she thought by the expression on Lord Kirkly's face that that was what he thought she was doing anyway, and she felt her heart sink!

She was certain that as soon as they arrived in Italy he would keep to his plan of disposing of her on the first ship that was going to England, and then she would be on her own.

During the day she tortured herself with the fear that Jules de Chalon would somehow find out on which ship she was sailing and when it left Genoa she would find him aboard.

She looked back at how persuasive he had been when he asked her to marry him and realised, as she had done already, how completely and utterly determined the Frenchmen were as a family that her money should be theirs.

At first she had been flattered by the compliments they paid her and the attention of three men who made it palpably clear that they wished only to please her.

Then because she was intelligent she realised that what appeared to be kindness was only a subtle way of getting her into their clutches, and she began to be frightened.

It was difficult to explain to anyone, even Lord Kirkly, how terrified she had been that they really would dope her to the point where she would not know what she was doing.

She would wake up and find herself married, and after that there would be no escape from the trap.

But she was not free of them yet, and she was well aware that in France the Chalons were a well-known family with an ancient title, who could command a great deal of respect.

The Police would readily search for her on their instructions and certainly would not listen to any protests she might make when they finally captured her.

As the day passed she had an irresistible impulse to hold on to Lord Kirkly as if he were a life-buoy in a dangerous sea, but her instinct told her that he was already to some extent regretting being inveigled into assisting her.

She was therefore terrified that if she upset him in any way, he might leave her earlier than he was planning to.

She was also aware, because she was perceptive, that his thoughts were not only with her, but with something else which had made him very angry.

When his face was in repose, she thought there was a grim look about the sides of his mouth and the squareness of his chin, and she admitted to herself that she was a little frightened of him.

There was something hard and ruthless about Lord Kirkly which she recognised as having derived from an awareness of his own importance and also as characteristic of a man who had fended for himself in a difficult and perhaps dangerous world.

"I would hate to be his enemy," Otila told herself.

She watched him from under her eyelashes, thinking he was an enigma she was unable to understand.

As he chatted to her during the long hours in the

train, she was aware of an anxiety that seemed to grow with every mile they covered, and it made her very tired.

"I think you ought to go to bed," Lord Kirkly said as if he knew what she was feeling.

As he spoke Bates came from the serving-pantry, where he had been sitting tactfully after they had had their dinner in the Drawing-Room.

"I think it's time, M'Lord," he said, "that I made up your bed."

It was then Otila begged Lord Kirkly once again to take what appeared to be the very comfortable bed in the adjoining room.

But not only Lord Kirkly, but also Bates told her not to worry.

It was the ingenious Bates who had managed to push two rows of seats together, cover them with cushions, then add pillows and blankets, which were fortunately provided in case the weather turned cold.

It made up what looked like a very comfortable soft bed.

When it was complete, Bates surveyed his handiwork with satisfaction and Lord Kirkly said with a smile:

"You see, you need not worry about me, Otila, and with Bates to look after me, I have no need of a woman to cosset me."

As he said the last words Otila remembered that Lord Kirkly had said he hated women, and it struck her for the first time that she was fortunate not to be alone in a private coach with the type of man who would have made her feel embarrassed if not actually afraid.

As it was, Lord Kirkly said in a voice he might have used to his sister:

"Go to bed, Otila, and do not worry. I am sure Bates has a magic idea that will deceive de Chalon, and once we are into Italy we shall be free of him and the rest of his fortune-seeking family."

"I hope you are right," Otila replied. "Good night My Lord, and thank you very, very much for being so kind to me."

She felt as she spoke there was a tremor in her voice which might embarrass Lord Kirkly because it was emotional.

She did not wait for his reply, but went into the sleeping carriage and shut the door.

When she was in bed, she said a little prayer that Lord Kirkly and Bates were right, and that when she left the train Jules de Chalon would not recognise her.

Then because she was actually exhausted by all that had happened, she fell asleep.

*   *   *

The train made one last stop in France early in the morning, and when an hour or two later Otila was dressed and came into the Drawing-Room for breakfast, it was to find Lord Kirkly reading a newspaper.

She looked at him in surprise, and as he rose to his feet he said:

"I see, as I rather expected, that the newspapers have reported that you are missing."

"How can they be aware of it so soon?" Otila asked in horror.

"I imagine," Lord Kirkly said, "that the Police

work hand-in-glove with the Journalists of the more sensational newspapers, and in both of those which Bates was able to buy early this morning they have made quite a dramatic story of your disappearance."

He spoke sarcastically and Otila, picking up the newspaper he was not reading but which was on the seat beside him, saw that on the front page there was a paragraph which had the headline:

HEIRESS MISSING FEARED KIDNAPPED

The story of her disappearance from the *Comte* de Chalon's house in the Champs-Élysées was made as dramatic as possible, and no reference was made to the fact that she had drugged the woman in charge of her and left her in the Café.

Instead, the *Comte* de Chalon had given an interview to a reporter saying that he was deeply perturbed since Miss Otila Ashe, who had recently inherited millions of American dollars from her grandfather, might have been spirited away by kidnappers intent on demanding a large ransom for her.

She read:

MISS ASHE, WHO HAS BEEN STAYING WITH US IN ORDER TO IMPROVE HER FRENCH, IS A VERY CHARMING YOUNG LADY OF WHOM MY WIFE AND I HAVE GROWN VERY FOND. IN FACT, IT IS NO SE-CRET THAT WE HOPE SHE MIGHT BECOME OUR DAUGHTER-IN-LAW. WE ARE THEREFORE EX-TREMELY ANXIOUS AS TO WHAT COULD HAVE HAPPENED TO HER, AND CAN ONLY PRAY THAT

SHE WILL BE RETURNED TO US UNHARMED AS
SOON AS POSSIBLE. . . .

The other newspaper reported that the Police had
an important clue which made them think that the
kidnappers might, in fact, be of the same nationality
as Miss Otila Ashe, and were intent on taking her to
England.

It finished by saying that the Channel ports were
being watched by the Police and enquiries were being
made of all the cross-Channel steamers.

After she had read what had been written, Otila
breathed out deeply, and then in a frightened little
voice, her eyes dark with fear, she said to Lord Kirkly:

"They will be watching for me when we reach the
frontier!"

Lord Kirkly looked at his watch.

"That will be in about ten minutes," he said.

Otila gave a little cry.

"What shall I do? Shall I hide?"

"Certainly not!" Lord Kirkly said. "You forget,
Otila, I have added you to my passport, and you are
my wife! But I certainly think you should put on these
extremely disfiguring spectacles and your hat with its
concealing veil."

"Of course, I forgot!" Otila cried.

Jumping up, she ran back into the Bedroom to do
as he had told her.

When she returned, Lord Kirkly smiled and said:

"You certainly look quite unattractive. In fact, I
think you are almost an insult to my good taste!"

Otila laughed as he meant her to do. Then he said:

"Sit down, Otila, and eat your breakfast. I promise you there need be no reason for alarm until we reach Milan, and Bates will then take charge."

Otila tried to obey him, but the food seemed to stick in her throat, and she could only manage to drink a little coffee before they arrived at the frontier.

It proved, however, nothing of an ordeal.

As Lord Kirkly had anticipated, the Italians were far more lax in the inspection of his passport than the French or the English would have been, and, even more, the Germans.

He also commanded their respect by being in a private coach, and after only a perfunctory glance at the passport he held out, the officials merely asked if he had anything to declare and accepted his reply of "Nothing," with a respectful bow.

Then the train moved on again and they were on Italian soil.

That, however, did not eliminate the danger of Jules de Chalon, who was travelling with them.

As some hours later they neared Milan, Lord Kirkly said:

"Now, Otila, you will do exactly what Bates had planned and make yourself look as if you were in pain."

Bates had already asked Otila if she had any powder with her, and she powdered her face until it looked white, and made dark lines under her eyes with a pencil, although it was doubtful if they would show behind her glasses.

As Bates had instructed her, she covered her head with a chiffon scarf and tied it round her neck, leaving as little of her face showing as possible.

She went back into the Drawing-Room and having put on the travelling-cape that belonged to Lord Kirkly, which looked somewhat austere, she sat on the sofa with her legs up and covered with a rug.

It was Bates who thought of informing the guard before they retired for the night that Lady Kirkly had unfortunately fallen down and sprained her ankle and was in considerable pain, while Otila remained unseen in the Bedroom.

Lord Kirkly explained in quite fluent Italian that on arrival at Milan they would require a wheel-chair to take her from the train to their carriage, and everything must be arranged so that she suffered as little discomfort as possible.

The guard promised to telegraph down the line, and Bates confirmed that everything was in order before they reached the huge terminus which, as Lord Kirkly said, would be conveniently crowded, and with any luck, by the time they left the train, Jules de Chalon would be far ahead of them.

A wheel-chair was brought to the carriage door, and making a great deal of fuss over carrying her so as not to jar her leg, Lord Kirkly and Bates lifted Otila out and settled her in the chair with a rug over her legs.

She bent her head as if in pain and put her hand over her eyes, not daring to look as they pushed her down the platform.

Only when she had been lifted again with great care into a closed carriage did she ask Lord Kirkly:

"Was he there? Could you see him?"

As they drove away, Bates following in another carriage with the luggage, Lord Kirkly said:

"I am quite certain we went undetected, but as you can imagine, Otila, I was too sensible to look about, but kept my eyes fixed on you as if I were worried, which of course I was, about you."

Otila gave a sigh of relief.

"What do we do now?" she asked.

"We are being very clever—at least I think so," Lord Kirkly said. "We are driving away from the station, then returning to catch the train that is leaving in about half an hour for Genoa."

Otila did not say anything, but she felt her spirits drop.

Lord Kirkly was determinedly sticking to his plan to be rid of her as soon as possible, and she longed to beg him to let her stay with him a little longer, perhaps a night at a Hotel. She knew, however, it was something she could not do.

Only when they were in the train leaving Milan for Genoa did she ask in a small voice:

"Supposing . . . there is . . . no ship? Or it is . . . full?"

"I think we will face that difficulty when we come to it," Lord Kirkly replied. "What is more important, Otila, is to get you home as quickly as possible, and for you to tell your uncle your version of what has been happening to you in France, before the *Comte* manages to tell his."

There was silence before Otila asked:

"Are you really thinking that the *Comte* will go to England to try to persuade my uncle that he should order me to marry one of his sons?"

"I would not be surprised," Lord Kirkly said. "But once you are at home, you can make it absolutely clear that you have no intention of marrying any of the Chalons, and also tell your uncle how badly they have behaved by trying to keep you a prisoner."

Otila looked unhappy. Then she said, still in a small voice:

"Perhaps . . . my uncle will not . . . listen to me."

"I am sure he will, but if not, you must go to one of your other relatives," Lord Kirkly said. "After all, it would be impossible in England to be pressured, as you would be in France, into a marriage which you dislike and have no intention of making. You must be assertive, Otila, which I am sure you can be, and if you are wise, I think you should see your father's Solicitor and tell him what happened to you while you were with the Chalons."

Otila did not reply; she merely looked worried and unhappy.

When they joined the train that was to carry them to Genoa, she took off the scarf from her head and discarded the cape which belonged to Lord Kirkly, and now was again looking extremely attractive in the blue travelling-gown in which she had left France.

It had been a very expensive garment, and without really meaning to, Lord Kirkly appreciated the smallness of her waist, and the manner in which the bodice of her gown fitted so neatly over her figure.

She was exceedingly pretty, in fact, lovely, but he told himself he had no interest in women and the sooner he could start on his journey to Tunis the better.

In fact, he had decided that when he finally disposed of Otila, he would leave Italy as soon as possible, having no wish to be involved with any Italian after his last encounter with the Ambassador in London.

Because she realised he was preoccupied and no longer thinking about her, Otila was silent. At the same time, she was feeling more and more apprehensive for herself.

It had never struck her until now that the *Comte* might make capital out of the fact that she had disappeared from his charge and would persuade her uncle, who she suspected would be only too willing to listen, that the best possible protection for her in the future was to be married.

Although it might be ridiculous, she had the feeling that once again she was being menaced, and there was nowhere she could go for safety where she could be free from men whose real interest lay not in her but in her money.

"What can I do? What can I do?" she asked herself.

There was no answer but the rumble of the wheels which were carrying her swiftly to Genoa, where she would lose Lord Kirkly.

Then without meaning to she began to pray that she had been right in thinking there might be no ship to take her, and she could stay with him if only for another one or two days rather than lose him altogether.

Then as if he knew what she was thinking Lord Kirkly said:

"Do stop worrying, Otila. I can feel it vibrating from you as you work yourself up to being afraid when there is no longer any need for fear."

"How can you be certain of that?" Otila asked.

"By using my common sense," he said sharply. "I have told you that I will make certain there is somebody on board to look after you, whom you can sit with so that you will not be at the mercy of any Tom, Dick, or Harry who wants to talk to you. And when you reach England, I will make sure that there is somebody to meet you at the port by sending your uncle a telegram as soon as your ship has left."

"Thank . . . you."

Then she gave a little cry.

"Supposing," she said, "when your telegram arrives, the *Comte* is already with Uncle Edward, and he offers to go to meet me himself? In that case he may . . . insist on my returning to . . . France with him."

"Now you are letting your imagination run riot," Lord Kirkly said in a tone of irritation. "You need not suppose anything of the sort, and surely your uncle will realise you have come home because you found things not as enjoyable in France as he had thought you would."

"I do not think Uncle Edward has much imagination."

"Well, I can hardly telegraph him to say that on no account is he to let the *Comte* de Chalon know of your arrival."

"I do not see why not."

"Very well," Lord Kirkly said after a moment's thought. "I will ask if he will meet you himself and on no account let anybody else know of your arrival until you can explain what happened. Will that satisfy you?"

He spoke crossly and Otila felt he would think her

extremely stupid and ungrateful if she made any more difficulties.

So she merely sat quietly without speaking and after a few minutes Lord Kirkly picked up his newspaper and she was sure he did not wish to be interrupted again.

Although they had taken the fast train, it was late in the evening before they arrived at Genoa, and Lord Kirkly was obliged to take Otila to a Hotel, where they could stay the night.

"I will make enquiries about a ship first thing in the morning," he said. "So have a good rest, and breakfast in your room. By the time you are dressed I will have some news for you."

He spoke cheerfully, but when Otila left him to go to bed she felt there was nothing to be cheerful about.

Lord Kirkly had engaged a Suite at the Hotel, but it was difficult to speak at all intimately while they were being waited on, and when dinner was over Otila had the feeling that he was eager to dispense with her presence.

She wanted to sit and talk to him, even if it was not about herself and her problems, but she found herself saying good night, and went to her Bedroom, feeling like a child who had been suddenly sent home from a party.

"After tomorrow I shall never see him again," she said. "I shall have to fight my own battles and rely on myself."

It was a depressing thought, for she was now feeling completely inadequate. She wanted to cling to Lord Kirkly and beg him even if it meant going down on her knees to let her stay with him a little longer.

Perhaps one of the Chalons would be waiting for her when she landed in England, or perhaps as she had feared the *Comte* had seen her uncle and persuaded him to approve her marriage to Jules.

If that happened, whom should she turn to for protection?

"I shall have to run away again," she told herself, and wondered whether it would be possible for her to go to America and find some of her unknown American relatives.

The whole idea was very frightening, and when she got into bed she could only shiver, as if it were cold.

Then she tried to tell herself she must be sensible. After all, she had been very lucky so far in finding Lord Kirkly and in getting out of France.

Perhaps there were other "Lord Kirklys" in the world, and if things became too intolerable in England, she would find one.

Then as she resolutely shut her eyes and told herself she must go to sleep she knew, however much she might dislike men, she would still like to stay with him because only then would she feel safe.

* * *

Lord Kirkly had a good night, waking early, as he usually did, and rang for Bates.

"Did you find out about the ships?" he asked after his valet had helped him dress.

"Yes, M'Lord. There's a P. and O. vessel due in

this morning on its way back from India, which will be leavin' this afternoon."

"Excellent, Bates!" Lord Kirkly exclaimed.

As he spoke he thought that nothing could be more fortunate, for there would certainly be some important Officer's wife returning from India, who could be persuaded to chaperon Otila until they reached England.

"I will send a telegram to her uncle after she has left," he told himself, "and it is a good idea to tell him to keep her arrival secret so that she will have a chance to inform him of the unspeakable way in which the Chalons have behaved."

He knew, however, that Otila's apprehension about being forced into marriage was not without foundation.

Until she was twenty-one she was under the guardianship of her uncle, and a guardian could give his consent to any marriage whether the bride wished it or not, and she would be bound to obey him.

"I cannot believe the man could be such a fool as not to realise that Otila is being married only for her money," Lord Kirkly said to himself.

At the same time he was sorry he could not speak to Otila's uncle personally and explain to him what she had gone through.

He wondered if he should write him a letter putting down every detail of what he had learnt.

Then he told himself that if he did so, he would become even more and more involved, and the sooner he could rid himself of Otila and concentrate on his own troubles the better.

"I want to get away," he said testily, and found himself saying it aloud without meaning to.

"Where's Your Lordship thinkin' of goin'?" Bates asked.

"I have not yet made up my mind," Lord Kirkly replied, "but I have no wish to stay in Italy."

"No, of course not, M'Lord."

Lord Kirkly thought it was impertinent of Bates to show that he knew the real reason, but there was nothing he could do about it, and Bates had been with him far too long and knew far too much not to be aware that at the moment all Italians were "tarred with the same brush" as far as he was concerned.

It was still quite early in the morning when he set off from the Hotel down to the harbour, but he was gratified to see that the P. & O. Liner was tied up at the Quay, and when he went aboard, the purser, looking smart and spruce, was ready in his office to receive enquiries.

Lord Kirkly introduced himself and said:

"I want to book the best cabin you have available for a young relative of mine who is returning to England from School. I should also be grateful if you could find somebody on board who would be willing to chaperon her during the voyage."

"That should not be difficult, My Lord," the purser said. "There are a number of ladies returning home from the East and I am sure any of them would be delighted to accommodate any relative of Your Lordship's."

He picked up a passenger list as he spoke and started to scrutinise it, and as he did so a steward came up beside him and whispered something in his ear.

"The Police!" the purser exclaimed audibly. "What do they want?"

"He's quite a Senior Official, sir."

The purser frowned and said to Lord Kirkly:

"I wonder if you will excuse me a moment, M'Lord, and perhaps you would be kind enough to look at the passenger list in case there is somebody whose name you recognise."

He handed him the list and went to the other window in his office, where Lord Kirkly could see a Senior Police Officer was waiting for him.

Almost without meaning to, he found himself listening to what was being said.

It was not too difficult, as the Italian Police Officer was speaking English.

"Is there, by any chance," the Officer was asking, "a cabin booked in the name of Miss Otila Ashe? If so, I would be obliged if you would take me to it immediately!"

"Why should I do that?" the purser asked.

"The young woman in question is wanted by the French Police. We should also be grateful if you would let us know of any unattached young woman who has booked with you under some other name."

"This is a very unusual procedure," the purser said evasively.

"I know that," the Italian Police Officer replied, "but the *Sûreté* in Paris is concerned over a million-airess who has disappeared, and they think she may have been kidnapped!"

"If she has been kidnapped, she is not likely to be travelling in this ship," the purser said with unanswerable logic.

"Well, those are our instructions, but of course she may be running away. Young women do that sometimes!"

The purser laughed.

"If they run, they usually have somebody running with them."

"That's true enough," the Italian Policeman replied, "especially if they're pretty!"

He laughed heartily, then said:

"Nevertheless, I will be calling again in a few hours to see if you have anything to tell me. In the meantime, I am off to notify the other ships in the harbour."

"Well, I hope you find your heiress," the purser said, "and if she is that well off, I would like to meet her!"

The two men laughed again. When the purser came back to him Lord Kirkly said, holding up the passenger list:

"I wonder if I could borrow this from you. I want to show it to my relative, who may easily recognise somebody on board. We are staying at the Hotel Royale, and I will communicate with you in a few hours. Is that all right?"

"Yes, of course, My Lord," the purser agreed, "and incidentally, what is your relative's name?"

Lord Kirkly did not hesitate.

"The same as mine," he said, "and I will give you full particulars on my return."

"Very well, M'Lord. I shall look forward to hearing

from you, and we shall be sailing at four o'clock this afternoon."

"Thank you very much."

With the passenger list in his hand Lord Kirkly got back into the carriage and returned to the Hotel.

Otila was waiting for him and as he walked into the Suite she looked at the expression on his face and said:

"Something has happened! What is it?"

Lord Kirkly threw the passenger list down onto the table before he said:

"The Chalons are being rather cleverer than we gave them credit for."

"What do you mean? What has happened?"

Lord Kirkly told her what he had overheard on the ship and she gave a cry of horror.

"They are determined to have me arrested. You realise what will happen? The Italian Police will hand me over to the French, and the French, whatever I may say, will deliver me to the *Comte.*"

"I am aware of that," Lord Kirkly said, "and I think the best thing we can do now is to go on immediately to Naples."

"But surely . . . the same thing will apply there?" Otila said hesitatingly.

Lord Kirkly was silent. Then he said:

"I suppose I might as well put a good face on it! I see I shall have to take you out of Europe before we can be free of the Police."

Otila's heart leapt, and Lord Kirkly would have been very obtuse if he had not realised there was a light in her eyes and an expression on her face that had not been there before.

"You will . . . take me with . . . you?"

"Only out of Europe!" he said sharply. "Then, when I can find a ship that is going to England and has not been warned to look out for you, I will put you on it."

"Yes, of course," Otila agreed. "But that does mean you will take me as far as Tunis, or wherever you are going."

Because she was so elated, Lord Kirkly suddenly felt angry.

"Dammit all," he said, "how the hell did I get mixed up in this mess? Your troubles have nothing to do with me! As I told you, I wish to go off on my own, and not be bedevilled by women!"

Because he spoke so angrily, Otila felt the tears come into her eyes.

"I am . . . sorry . . . I am truly sorry . . . but I was frightened . . . of what might . . . happen to me . . . on that ship . . . and I was right! Although we did not know it was a trap, and if we had walked into it, I would have been lost!"

Because she spoke so humbly, Lord Kirkly suddenly felt as if he had struck out at something small and vulnerable that could not defend itself.

"Luckily you were saved," he said, "so we can just tear up that sailing list and forget about the P. & O. Liner."

Otila gave a deep sigh.

Then as she sat down on a chair, feeling as if her legs would no longer carry her, she said:

"I think the . . . best thing would be for me to go into . . . a Convent for . . . a little while. I may not take the veil, but I am sure if I paid them enough they

93

would . . . keep me there and I would be . . . safe . . . and you would not have to . . . think about me anymore."

"I do not think that is at all a practical idea," Lord Kirkly replied. "Firstly, I doubt if any Convent would take you in such circumstances; secondly you are not a Catholic, and thirdly—I do not really think you are suited to a life of prayer and seclusion!"

Now there was a touch of laughter in his voice and as Otila looked up at him and realised he was no longer angry, she blinked away her tears.

"I know it has . . . made you . . . angry," she said, "but I am so . . . happy that I can . . . stay with you a little . . . longer!"

chapter five

THEY arrived in Naples very late in the evening after a somewhat uncomfortable journey, which made Otila feel apprehensive that Lord Kirkly would be angrier with her than ever.

'It is my fault he is having to put up with all this,' she thought, and tried to make herself as pleasant as she could, hoping that somehow she could amuse him when he wanted to talk.

She had the feeling that he was resenting more and more the fact that they must move from pillar to post simply because she was being searched for by the Police.

She felt by the time they reached Naples not only

tired but so apologetic that she had run out of words.

Fortunately the Hotel they booked into was large and luxurious and, as usual, Lord Kirkly took the best Suite available, which had comfortable Bedrooms for each of them.

In the morning when Otila awoke it was to find that Lord Kirkly had already gone out and she was sure he had gone to discover what ships there were to take them out of Italy.

As long as she could travel as his wife she knew that she was safe.

At the same time, she could not help a quiver of fear whenever she thought of Jules de Chalon pursuing her, and perhaps by guessing in some uncanny way where they had gone, he was ahead of them.

When Lord Kirkly returned to the Suite he was smiling, and she jumped up from the breakfast-table to ask:

"Is everything all right? I was worried when I found you had left so early."

"It was not early for me!" Lord Kirkly said in a lofty way. "But I admit to having had only a cup of coffee before I left and I am ready for breakfast."

Bates had already ordered it for him and he sat down at the table to say to Otila:

"Good news! There is an excellent ship leaving tomorrow for Tunis. I have booked some quite adequate accommodation on it, and from Africa there should be no difficulty in finding a ship which will carry you to England."

Otila did not speak for a moment, but then she asked:

"What . . . will . . . you do?"

"Explore," Lord Kirkly said. "As I have told you, I have friends in Tunis, and I also want to see some of the Roman remains which I am told are very interesting."

Otila did not speak.

She was thinking how exciting it would be if she could go with him.

As if he were aware of her thoughts, he said quickly:

"I have, however, something interesting for us to do this afternoon, which I think will amuse you."

"What is that?" Otila asked.

"I met quite by chance as I went to the harbour, an old friend, who is very important."

Otila listened attentively, and Lord Kirkly went on.

"His name is Antonio Caruso and he is the Champion Fencer of Italy."

Otila's eyes lit up.

"I would love to meet him!"

"That is what you are going to do. He tells me that since I was last here he has a new house onto which he has built a room for his pupils, which fulfils all his dreams of what should be the right background for the most graceful and certainly one of the most intricate sports in the world."

"I agree with you," Otila said. "I think fencing is fascinating, and I believe you, My Lord, are a very good fencer."

Lord Kirkly smiled.

"I try to be."

"I was told," Otila said, "that you would be a champion fencer if you would only agree to enter competitions."

"That may be true," Lord Kirkly agreed, "and although I enjoy fencing, I would not wish to make an exhibition of myself! Nevertheless, if it would amuse you, I dare say Caruso and I could arrange a little exhibition this afternoon."

"I would love that!" Otila exclaimed. "I would find it very, very exciting!"

There was no doubting the sincerity with which she spoke, and it flashed through his mind that it was very different from the rather affected way in which other women who had watched him fence had acclaimed his expertise.

He knew it was because they did not really understand the art of fencing and had no idea of the subtlety of every move, every position.

"The Italians are good fencers," he said conversationally as Bates brought his breakfast and set it down on the table in front of him, "but on the whole I believe there is no one to equal the Austrians."

Otila looked surprised.

"I would have expected you to say the French."

"They are too emotional," Lord Kirkly replied. "One needs a cool, clear head and an almost impersonal approach to be a good fencer."

"It will be thrilling for me to watch you," Otila said.

"And Antonio Caruso!" Lord Kirkly added. "He is exceptional and by far the best teacher in the whole of Europe!"

When they had finished breakfast, Otila would have liked to see a little of Naples, but Lord Kirkly thought it was too dangerous.

"There is no point in taking any risks," he said. "I think it is doubtful that Jules de Chalon will come here from Genoa. He is far more likely to have gone to Rome, but one cannot be sure."

"No . . . of course not," Otila said.

She went to the window and looked out over the walls of the City and beyond the blue of the sea.

"It is very lovely!" she exclaimed. "I have always been told that Naples has a special light about it which is different from other Cities."

"Someday perhaps you will come to stay here," Lord Kirkly said. "As it happens, I have a Villa farther along the coast which belonged to my grandmother and there, as she was in ill-health, she spent the last remaining years of her life. As we are leaving tomorrow, there is no time for us to go there, but perhaps on my way back I might stay a few days and see if the place is being kept in proper order."

The way he spoke made Otila acutely aware that she would not be with him.

She wondered what he would say if she begged him to take her to the Villa for a few days first before they left for Tunis.

Then she reminded herself that she was just an encumbrance, someone who had thrust herself upon him, and while he had shown her a great deal of kindness he had no wish to be further involved with her than was necessary.

Lord Kirkly came to stand beside her at the window.

Then he said in a somewhat dry voice:

"Very romantic! Certainly somewhere, Otila, where you must spend your honeymoon, when you have one."

"You know I have no wish to be married or to

spend a honeymoon with any man!" Otila retorted sharply.

Lord Kirkly laughed.

Once again he was reminded of a small tiger-cat spitting at what she disliked.

"At the same time, you are a woman, Otila, whether you like it or not, and a woman needs a man to look after her. You, in particular, need protection, and who better to give it to you than a husband?"

"How can you talk of anything so unpleasant and be so unkind to me?" Otila asked. "You know I am cursed by my money so that whatever a man says to me, however pleasant he may be, I shall always think that he is really in love with my bank balance."

"That is being cynical and extremely stupid!" Lord Kirkly said. "I think now the real solution to your problem is quite simple—you must go to America and find your American relations! I expect there will be several millionaires amongst them who have quite enough money of their own without bothering about yours."

He thought to himself as he spoke that that really was a perfect solution and one he should have thought of before.

In fact, he should have tried to book her passage on a ship bound for New York rather than one to England.

Then as he looked down at Otila and saw the expression on her small face and the darkness of her eyes, he remembered how young and inexperienced she was and how easily she became afraid.

"The whole situation is ridiculous!" he told himself

irritably. "How can this child, for she is little more, look after herself? It would be quite impossible for her to deal with fortune-hunters, who will undoubtedly pop up like mushrooms wherever she goes."

He knew the reports in the newspapers would not have helped the situation, and he could picture in his mind a great number of other Frenchmen who would be interested in meeting Otila, knowing that a bride with a large dowry was a necessity for any marriage they made.

In England the postion was very much the same.

Lord Kirkly could think without any effort of half a dozen young aristocrats whose ancestral homes and large estates were definitely in need of an injection of American dollars and who in consequence would find Otila a fascinating proposition.

"Dammit all," he swore to himself, "what can the girl do? Unless she can somehow contrive to be anonymous in a country where she is not known."

As this was obviously an impossibility, he stood beside Otila, looking at the sunlit beauty in front of them and feeling that her future was a complicated problem that was both dark and menacing.

Otila gave a deep sigh.

"As we have so little time left," she said, "please do not let us talk about my marriage. The whole idea frightens me, and sometimes I wish I could just . . . die!"

Lord Kirkly would have spoken, but she went on quickly.

"At the same time, I do want to live! I know there are many exciting places in the world I long to see and many that, like you, I would like to explore. Surely it is possible for me to do so without having to be married to someone who would not understand and would perhaps laugh at me for wishing to be adventurous?"

"Of course there are men who will love you for yourself," Lord Kirkly said, "but unfortunately the right sort of man does not usually want to have a wife who is very much richer than himself. So you have to face the fact, Otila, that a lot of men who call themselves Gentlemen will avoid you simply because unlike the Chalons, they do not want your money, which would embarrass them."

As he spoke he realised this was a new idea that had not struck Otila before, and she said after a moment:

"What you are really saying is that I shall have to accept the type of man who marries me for money, or else become an old maid."

Lord Kirkly thought it was quick of her to see the point so clearly and he said soothingly:

"It is not quite as bad as that, but I think it is something you should consider, and perhaps not condemn all men as fortune-hunters as you are doing at the moment."

"You are making me feel more and more . . . afraid of the . . . future," Otila said in a childlike voice.

"I am sorry. I have no wish to do that," Lord Kirkly said. "I am just trying to think of what is best for you. Perhaps I should write to your uncle and suggest that he take better care of you than he has done up until now."

"I very much doubt if he will listen to you," Otila said. "I have already told you he finds me a bore, and I have interrupted the quiet, peaceful life he was living before Papa died."

She paused for a moment before she said:

"I am certain my aunt and he both feel that the sooner I am married and off their hands the better they will like it, and it will not matter to them to whom!"

"But if you do not wish to go back to England, then where can you go?" Lord Kirkly asked.

Now because he was finding the problem tiresome he spoke sharply.

Otila gave a little cry.

"Please, do not let us bicker. Let us forget it for today. It is so lovely to be with you, and there are so many things you can tell me that I want to know. There is no point in our being upset and ruining everything by talking about my beastly marriage, or my horrible money! So let us forget them."

She clasped her hands together.

"Tell me everything you know about Tunis so that as the ship takes me farther and farther away from you I can imagine you climbing over some beautiful half-ruined theatre or standing against some exquisite Ionic pillars silhouetted against the sky."

"I cannot describe Tunis to you," Lord Kirkly replied with a smile, "until I have been there. Instead, I will tell you what I found in Greece, and if you like, what I felt when I first saw the Acropolis and after a journey by sea saw the cliffs of Delphi shining above me."

*   *   *

It was two hours later before Lord Kirkly realised he had been talking of his travels in a way he had never done before to any woman.

Otila had hardly spoken except to ask him intelligent questions that he had answered, but had sat with her eyes on his, listening to every word in a way he found not only flattering but intriguing.

He had never known a woman whose eyes were so expressive and which told him without speaking how much what he was saying excited and in a way inspired her.

He could read her thoughts almost as if she spoke them aloud, and he knew that in a strange way she was reading his and at the same time she knew it was not only what he had seen but what he had felt that mattered.

Half an hour before luncheon Bates brought in a bottle of champagne for Lord Kirkly.

As he poured out a glass for his master and one for Otila, it broke the spell which had held her enchanted to the point where she felt as if Lord Kirkly had carried her away into a world that she had always known was there, but never had it expressed to her before, either in words or in books.

Then she gave a deep sigh as she said:

"All you have told me has made me aware of how fully you have lived, which is something I have not even begun to do."

"I do not think that is true," Lord Kirkly said. "You may not have been to the places I have seen, but you have thought and felt, and that is just as important as travelling by land or sea."

"I would like to think that," Otila said. "At the same time, I realise how lucky you are and it makes me very envious."

"One day you will do it all yourself," Lord Kirkly said reassuringly. "After all, it is something you can afford to do, whereas most people, as we both know, are handicapped by being too poor to be able to travel."

For a moment she looked at him, then as she looked away he saw the darkness in her eyes and knew that once again she was thinking there was no one to go with her except some husband, who might be more interested in throwing her money away on a racecourse, or losing it in a Casino.

Then as he felt he could not bear to hear this all over again, Lord Kirkly rose from the chair in which he had been sitting and walked to the window.

To change the subject he said:

"I suggest we order a special luncheon this afternoon before we go to visit my friend and talk about fencing."

"Yes, of course," Otila said, "that will be very exciting."

She went from the room, and when she had gone, Bates came back to pour out another glass of champagne for Lord Kirkly and bring him a menu from which to choose luncheon.

"I understand, M'Lord," Bates said, "that we'll be leavin' tomorrow mornin'. There's one or two things I has to get for Your Lordship before we sets off."

"Very well, Bates," Lord Kirkly replied. "Get anything you want, but do not forget I shall need some comfortable walking shoes."

"I've already thought of that, M'Lord!"

Then as Lord Kirkly took a sip of his champagne Bates said:

"I've been thinkin' about Miss Otila, M'Lord, and wondering 'ow she'll manage by 'erself, makin' the journey home alone from Tunis."

"She will manage," Lord Kirkly said sharply. "There will be people on board only too pleased to chaperon her, and I will make certain that they do so competently."

"I think it would be a mistake all the same, M'Lord, for them to know who she really is, seein' as 'ow the papers are full of the story of the missing millionairess."

Lord Kirkly looked at him.

"Are you telling me it is in the Italian newspapers this morning?"

"Yes, M'Lord. Quite a story they're making out of it, and 'ow the Police of almost every country in Europe has been notified that she's missing."

Lord Kirkly tightened his lips.

Then because he had no wish to discuss it, he said:

"Well, she is safe enough at the moment, and we must think of some way before she leaves Tunis by which she can travel under another name."

"In which case, M'Lord, she'll want a new passport."

As if Bates knew this was a parting shot to which there was no reply, he left the room.

It was then that Lord Kirkly told himself that the

situation was growing worse, and there was nothing he could do about it.

"Why, in God's name, did I allow myself to become involved in this mess?" he asked.

He thought it would have been far more sensible if he had followed his instincts from the very beginning and left Otila to her fate.

*　　*　　*

Otila was in extremely high spirits as they drove away from the Hotel to visit Antonio Caruso.

She had made up her mind that after the exciting morning she had spent with Lord Kirkly listening to his adventures, she would not allow anything to spoil their luncheon.

She therefore talked animatedly and amusingly of her impressions of France and of living with a French family, making Lord Kirkly laugh at the little meannesses that were shown towards the servants and the other employees.

She also made fun of the manner in which they extolled their "blue blood" and their aristocratic lineage, at the same time taking every advantage of making a "little bit on the side" if it was possible to do so.

Because Otila was observant and too quick-witted for people to "pull the wool over her eyes," she made Lord Kirkly laugh and laugh again at the French pride which was very shallow when it came to a question of francs.

Now as they left the Hotel, Lord Kirkly found

himself thinking how attractive she looked in a summer gown of white trimmed with *broderie anglaise* and velvet ribbons.

The same ribbon skillfully ornamented her hat which was so *chic* that it could only have come from the Rue de la Paix, and the same could be said of her gloves and her shoes.

It was unusual for any girl to be so expensively dressed; at the same time Lord Kirkly had to admit that Otila's taste was faultless.

While everything she wore was *haute couture,* she was not over-dressed for her age, and it was obvious that everything she put on was a fitting frame for her beauty.

There was no doubt that she was beautiful, and once again Lord Kirkly was thinking that Nature had been over-abundant in giving her riches as well.

Antonio Caruso's house was high up above the City, not far from the Palaces of the Grandees of Naples.

It was not large, but as they approached it they could see how a wing had been built onto it which Lord Kirkly knew was the Fencing School, as had been described to him by his friend.

Antonio Caruso, who was waiting for them, greeted them effusively, then obviously eager to show off his new possession, he led them from the house into the new building, which at first glance was certainly very impressive.

It was, Lord Kirkly thought with his experienced eye, of exactly the right dimensions and the decoration was certainly unique.

The walls were covered with foils of every sort and description and they made together with masks, gloves, and other paraphernalia incidental to fencing, an unusual and extremely attractive pattern.

On one side as they entered were modern foils, épées, and sabres, and on the opposite side, as Antonio Caruso pointed out, were the antique weapons which he had collected all his life, including some of the first masks, invented in 1780.

Lord Kirkly walked round admiring everything.

Then as he and Otila sat down in comfortable arm-chairs, Antonio produced a bottle of golden wine with which he insisted they must drink his health.

"This is a new venture, My Lord," he said, "in which I need your good wishes and your good will, and I feel sure you will help me by telling your friends in London about me."

"I will certainly do that," Lord Kirkly agreed, "and I will send you as many pupils as possible. I know of nobody, and this is the truth, Antonio, who could teach a young man the finer points of fencing as well as you can."

The Italian was delighted, then as Lord Kirkly and Otila raised their glasses to the toast, he thanked them very eloquently and volubly and insisted on drinking their health in return.

"There is something else I want to show Your Lordship . . ." he began to say, when a servant came to his side to say in an audible whisper:

"The *Duc* di Oporto has arrived, *Signor,* with another gentleman!"

Antonio Caruso was apologetic.

"Forgive me," he said, "but the *Duc* said he might be calling today to collect a foil I have mended for him, but I did not expect him quite so early. Please make yourselves comfortable until I return."

"Do not worry about us," Lord Kirkly said as the Italian hurried from the room.

Otila rose from her chair.

"He has arranged all this very cleverly," she said, "and I can see that some of these new foils are quite different from any I have seen before."

"Have you seen many?" Lord Kirkly asked in surprise.

Otila was just about to reply, when suddenly there was a commotion at the door by which the Italian had just left and a man came into the School like a whirlwind.

He was smartly dressed, with dark hair, and was obviously Italian, but at the moment his cheeks were flushed and there was an expression on his face which made Otila stare at him in surprise as he seemed to run rather than walk towards Lord Kirkly.

"So you are here, My Lord!" he said in excellent English, but with a decided accent. "When I heard you had left London, I knew you had run away from me, and I was determined I would catch up with you sooner or later!"

As the Italian seemed almost to spit the words at him, Lord Kirkly, who was sitting back in his armchair did not move, but merely said in a dry, almost drawling voice:

"I was not running away, Your Excellency, but I have no reason to think we have any need to communicate with each other."

"I have every reason to communicate with you!" the Italian replied furiously. "You have behaved abominably! You have insulted me, taken advantage of me in my absence, and I consider I am entitled to an apology."

"That is a debatable point," Lord Kirkly replied, still in his slow, rather bored voice, which Otila felt must be very irritating to the already irate Italian.

She was standing behind him, as he was facing Lord Kirkly, and there was only a table with the bottle of wine on it between them.

Although she could not see the Italian's face, she could feel that his whole body from his shoulders downwards was pulsating with a furious anger which she was sure was explosive.

"And now," the Italian said, "now is the moment when I can take my revenge!"

"Are you suggesting that we fight a duel?" Lord Kirkly asked. "I cannot believe Your Excellency would insist on anything that was so detrimental to your wife's reputation!"

"Do not speak of my wife!" the Italian shouted. "It is you who have ruined her reputation! It is you who have made me a laughingstock in the Social World, and it is you, My Lord, who shall pay and pay dearly!"

As he spoke he stretched out his hand and snatched from the wall the nearest foil within reach.

"I have already asked you," Lord Kirkly said without moving, "if you intend that we should fight a duel."

"There will be no duel!" the Italian replied. "I know

111

your reputation as a swordsman, but I intend while I have you at my mercy to make sure you are unable to embrace my wife or any other woman for a very long time!"

He waved the foil menacingly in the air as he said:

"I intend to maim you, Kirkly, and what could be more convenient than that you should be at this moment, a 'sitting target,' as you English say, and that is exactly how I want you!"

As he spoke he kicked the table which stood between them to one side, upsetting the bottle of wine.

With a sensation of horror in her heart Otila realised the Italian was about to pierce Lord Kirkly with the foil while he sat weaponless and entirely defenceless.

Spontaneously she swiftly turned and snatched another foil from the wall.

Then as the Italian took a step towards Lord Kirkly, who still had not moved from the chair in which he was sitting, she leapt in front of him.

"On guard, Signor!" she cried, and lunged towards him so that to save his breast from being pierced the Italian was bound to parry her stroke.

"Out of my way, *Signora!* This has nothing to do with you."

"I cannot allow you, *Signor,* to be so unsporting as to attack an unarmed man!" Otila replied breathlessly.

She lunged at him again and forced him to defend himself, parrying each stroke she made, until suddenly Otila was not standing alone and with a leap of her heart she realised that Lord Kirkly had joined her and that now he too held a foil in his hand.

Then as she would have moved aside to let him take over as he obviously intended to, she lowered her guard and the Italian's foil pierced her right arm above the elbow and she gave a little cry of pain.

It was then that Lord Kirkly said angrily:

"If you want a fight, Your Excellency, you shall have one, but with me, and I intend to teach you a lesson you richly deserve!"

As Otila put her left hand over the wound on her arm and moved to one side to stand with her back to the wall, the two men were fighting fiercely.

It was a short battle and ended with Lord Kirkly with brilliant expertise, forcing the foil out of his opponent's hand.

He was therefore left weaponless while the point of Lord Kirkly's foil was pressed against his heart.

Just for a moment the two men glared at each other, and then Lord Kirkly said:

"Go home, Your Excellency, and stop making a fool of yourself! When you have calmed down, you will realise that if you had injured me, as you intended, it would have meant the end of your Diplomatic career."

The Italian was beaten and he knew it.

With an expression on his face of justified anger that was indescribable, he turned and walked from the room, and Lord Kirkly, putting his foil down on a chair, turned towards Otila.

"Has he hurt you?" he asked.

"N-no . . . it is all right," she tried to say.

Then as he reached her and saw the blood dripping

113

from her wound onto her white gown, she fainted in his arms.

* * *

Otila opened her eyes and found she was lying on her bed in the Hotel and Bates was beside her.

"Are you all right, Miss?" he asked as he saw she was conscious. "His Lordship's tryin' to get a Doctor, but I've cleaned your wound, an' it's stopped bleeding, although you've lost a lot of blood."

Otila did not speak, but as if he knew what she wanted, Bates brought her a cool drink, and lifting her head, held it to her lips.

Vaguely she remembered being carried to the carriage by Lord Kirkly and that he had his arm around her as they had driven back to the Hotel.

There he had carried her up the stairs and she must have fainted again with the movement because she did not remember anything after that.

She looked down at her arm and saw that it was bandaged, while a lace cover hid her gown with the bloodstains on it.

She felt faint and limp, and although she supposed she could get up and undress, it was too much effort to suggest it.

Then, as she shut her eyes, she heard Lord Kirkly's voice and opened them again.

"I have sent a porter for the nearest Doctor," she heard him say to Bates.

Then he came to her side.

He took her hand in his and said:

"How do you feel?"

"I—I am . . . all right," she said weakly.

"I suppose you realise that you saved me from being very much more severely damaged than you are, and I am very grateful."

"He . . . he must be . . . m-mad!" Otila whispered.

There was a little twist to Lord Kirkly's lips as he said:

"He has some grounds for his behaviour. At the same time, he was extremely unsporting, and should have fought me, if that was what he wished, in the proper manner."

"I . . . suppose he did not do that because he . . . knew that you would . . . win!" Otila said.

She tried to smile as she spoke the words, but her voice sounded very weak and Lord Kirkly said sharply to Bates:

"Go to see if there is any sign of the Doctor! How can it take so long to get one?"

"I-it . . . is only . . . a . . . scratch," Otila managed to say.

"It might have been worse," Lord Kirkly agreed. "At the same time, it was exceedingly brave of you."

Because he was praising her, Otila felt a warm feeling welling up inside her breast, and she looked up at him to say:

"Was the lady . . . over whom you were . . . fighting very . . . very . . . beautiful?"

Despite himself, Lord Kirkly smiled. Then he said:

"Not as beautiful as you, Otila, and that is the truth!"

Otila's eyes widened for a moment.

Then as she looked at him, his face near to hers, his eyes with a kind expression in them she had never seen before, she knew that she loved him.

chapter six

OTILA stirred a little restlessly and turned over again.

Lord Kirkly, who had been reading in an armchair just outside the door of her Bedroom, rose and went to her bedside.

There was just enough light for him to see that while her eyes were closed her lips were moving, and she was obviously, as the Doctor had expected, running a fever.

"I do not think it will be serious, My Lord," he had added, "but wounds like this, especially from a fencing foil which is not hygienically clean, often induce a fever and she may become slightly delirious."

"You are sure it is not serious?" Lord Kirkly had asked hastily.

The Doctor shook his head.

"Only somewhat painful, and the *Signora* has lost a lot of blood. But she is young, strong, and very beautiful, and will be all right in a day or two."

He looked with a smile as he spoke not at Lord Kirkly but at Otila, and it was obvious that he greatly admired her.

He then went with Lord Kirkly into another room and said:

"It will be difficult to get anybody immediately to nurse your wife, My Lord, but if you insist, I will try."

"Thank you, I can manage," Lord Kirkly replied. "My valet, who has travelled with me all over the world, is used to fevers and very adept at bandaging wounds."

"I have already given Her Ladyship a soothing potion which will make her sleep," the Doctor said. "If she wakes in the night and is restless, you can repeat the dose."

He handed Lord Kirkly a glass bottle, promised to call as early as possible in the morning, and left.

Lord Kirkly had gone back into the Bedroom to find Otila was already half-asleep from the effects of the drug.

As the Doctor had been so long in arriving, Bates had fetched two of the chambermaids to undress her and put her to bed.

The warm-hearted Italian women had exclaimed in horror at the blood on her gown, and had been very careful not to disturb her wounded arm more than they could help, as they put her into one of her pretty nightgowns.

Now with her hair falling over her shoulders, she looked very young and little more than a child as she threw her head restlessly from side to side on her pillow.

Lord Kirkly put his hand on her forehead, and finding as he expected that it was hot, he guessed she was running a temperature.

He thought it would be best to give her a second dose of the soothing potion the Doctor had prescribed, but before he could find the bottle which Bates had left on the dressing table, Otila started to speak.

"How . . . can I . . . escape? How can . . . I get away? I cannot . . . stay . . . here!"

The words came abruptly from between her lips, and there was a note of fear in her voice which Lord Kirkly recognised.

He knew she had gone back in her mind to the time when she was trying to escape from the Chalon house in Paris, and he said quietly:

"You have escaped, Otila. You are quite safe! Quite, quite safe!"

She was quiet for a moment and he hoped she had fallen asleep again.

Then, as if she were moving on in time, she said:

"We are . . . safe! We have . . . got away and he will not . . . find me in . . . Italy!"

Lord Kirkly knew then she was thinking of how, when they crossed the frontier from France to Italy, they thought they had got free of Jules de Chalon, only to find the Police were already investigating the ships sailing from Genoa.

He left her bedside and crossed the room to pick up the Doctor's medicine bottle from the table and the small glass that stood beside it.

As he did so Otila, turning restlessly again, said in a different voice from what she had used before:

"Please . . . God . . . let me stay with him . . . a little longer. Please . . . God . . . I cannot be . . . alone. I am . . . frightened . . . very . . . very frightened . . . please . . . please . . . let me . . . stay!"

Lord Kirkly realised she was praying, and he put the bottle down by her bedside before he said quietly:

"There is nothing to frighten you, Otila. You are safe—do you understand? You are safe and you are here with me."

As if his words reached her, she put out her hand unexpectedly and clutched hold of the revers of his coat.

"You are . . . with me?" she asked. "You have . . . not left . . . me?"

"I am here," Lord Kirkly said in a deep voice. "I will look after you, and you are safe—with me— perfectly safe!"

She gave a little murmur such as a child might have done.

Then as he put his arm around her to raise her head against him, she said in an almost normal voice:

"I am safe . . . with . . . you!"

Lord Kirkly held her close against him until he realised she had fallen deeply asleep.

He lay her down very gently on the pillow and left the glass of medicine untouched beside the bottle.

He had the feeling as he moved back to his armchair in the Sitting-Room that what he had said to her was

more soothing than anything the Doctor could pre-
scribe.

*   *   *

The following morning Otila was still running a
temperature and it was high, as the Doctor said was
only to be expected.

The wound on her arm was slightly inflamed, but
there was no need, the Doctor said, to worry about
it.

"Just keep your wife quiet for a few days, My
Lord," he ordered. "Give her plenty of liquids to drink
and persuade her, if possible, to take a little nourishing
soup, or anything which is easy to digest. We will
soon have her on her feet and looking more beautiful
than ever!"

Lord Kirkly thanked him for his services, and when
he had gone he called Bates into the Sitting-Room.

"I think, Bates," he said, "it is important that we
should leave here as soon as possible."

"Where's Your Lordship thinkin' of goin' to?"

"To my grandmother's Villa. I have a feeling that
with the Doctor talking of Miss Otila's beauty it would
be dangerous if people in Naples realised that until
now I have never been married. It might conceivably
make the Police curious."

"I thought o' that meself," Bates said, "but I didn't
like to alarm Your Lordship. But now I 'ears they're
making enquiries in the City."

Lord Kirkly's lips tightened but he did not say
anything, and Bates went on:

121

"Of course, M'Lord, they'll be lookin' for Miss Ashe, but that'll not stop them from putting two and two together, and makin' five!"

"I will take her to the Villa," Lord Kirkly said. "You leave immediately to tell them I am on my way, and make sure that every possible comfort is waiting for Miss Otila, so that she is not more disturbed than is absolutely necessary by the move or the journey."

"I'll do that, M'Lord," Bates said.

He moved away and Lord Kirkly, having looked into Otila's Bedroom to see that she was still asleep, picked up the morning newspapers.

He found, and it made him frown, that they were still running the story about the search for the missing heiress, and Otila's fortune increased every time it was mentioned.

There was nothing he could do except hope, as he had said to Bates, that no one would think it strange for a man who had been known to be an avowed bachelor to have arrived from France with a very beautiful young girl purporting to be his wife.

He feared that it seemed odd that there had been no announcement of a large and fashionable wedding, which is what would have been expected if he had given up his much-valued freedom.

Otila actually remembered nothing of the journey she made wrapped in blankets, lying full length on the back seat of a comfortable carriage while Lord Kirkly sat on the small seat opposite her with his back to the horses.

She saw nothing of the beautiful scenery along the coast, with Vesuvius looming high on one side of them and the vivid blue of the sea on the other.

Instead, a long time later she opened her eyes to stare in surprise at a room she had never seen before.

It was certainly much more beautiful than the one she had occupied at the Hotel, which she vaguely remembered as being rather nondescript and unattractive.

Now she found herself lying in a large bed with white muslin curtains falling on either side of her from a golden corola of angels, which touched the high ceiling.

On her left she could look through a large bow window and see the tops of pine trees, and beyond them a stretch of vivid Madonna blue, which she thought must be the Mediterranean.

Near at hand the room in which she was lying was all white, except for several exquisitely beautiful Venetian glass mirrors, and a Venetian chandelier that hung from the ceiling.

There was a picture of Venus with cupids on the wall, which she thought was very lovely. It was the only patch of colour, since even the rugs on the floor were all white, as was the rest of the furniture.

She lay staring around her, wondering where she could be.

Then with a sudden constriction of her heart she thought perhaps Lord Kirkly had sent her away and she had lost him.

The idea was so frightening that she tried to sit up in bed, but the movement brought a sharp pain to her

123

arm, which made her give a little cry.

As she did so Lord Kirkly came in from the balcony outside her window, where he had been sitting.

Otila looked at him for a moment, then her eyes seemed to fill her face as she exclaimed:

"You are . . . here . . . you are . . . really here! I thought I . . . had lost you!"

"I have been here all the time, Otila," Lord Kirkly said, "while you have been sleeping the clock round. Now that you are awake, I feel sure you would like something to drink, and perhaps to eat."

"I was afraid . . . when I saw this . . . strange room that . . . you had . . . sent me . . . away."

Otila was voicing her thoughts and found it difficult to take in what he was saying to her.

"I have not sent you anywhere," Lord Kirkly said, sitting down on the bed beside her, "but we have both moved from the Hotel into the Villa I told you about that belonged to my grandmother."

He realised as he spoke that Otila was looking at him with a happiness in her eyes that told him better than anything else that her fever was over and she was now herself again.

"You must hurry and get well, Otila," he said. "There are many things here that my grandmother collected which I know will interest and delight you. Greek statues, some very beautiful pictures, and other treasures which I had no idea, or else I had forgotten, that she possessed."

"Y-you . . . will show them . . . to me?"

"That is what I am looking forward to doing," Lord Kirkly said. "Bates tells me that your wound is healing

124

quickly and the inflammation has almost gone."

Otila looked down at her arm almost as if she had forgotten about it. Then she said:

"He . . . he will not . . . touch you again?"

"The Ambassador?" Lord Kirkly questioned. "No, of course not! He made a fool of himself, and I am sure by this time he realises it."

He paused. Then he put out his hand to cover one of Otila's and said:

"The story might have been quite difficult if it had not been for you."

"He . . . meant to . . . maim you!"

The words were only a whisper, but Lord Kirkly heard them and said quickly:

"He behaved in an uncontrolled and uncivilised manner, but we do not want to think about it now. What I would like to know is how you learnt to fence."

Otila smiled.

"Papa taught me many years ago, because he enjoyed it so much."

"It is something I would never have expected you to know how to do."

"I was . . . good enough to give . . . Papa a sporting fight . . . even though he always . . . beat me."

"You are full of surprises, Otila," Lord Kirkly remarked, "and I want to hear a great deal more about your talents. But first I am going to order you something to eat and drink."

He rose to open the door and called for Bates.

Then he went for a short walk in the garden of the Villa, while he knew that Otila was being attended to by the Italian maid-servants, who were very excited at having visitors to stay after being left alone and unnoticed for so many years.

The Villa was in fact so beautiful, and the garden such a riot of colour, that Lord Kirkly chided himself for having neglected it for so long.

He was, however, well aware that the problem of Otila was at the moment more important than anything else.

The fact that they were still in Italy might prove dangerous if the newspapers continued to publicise the search for her which, according to what they called "reliable sources," was taking place all over Europe.

Lord Kirkly had just read:

WHEN THE COMTE DE CHALON WAS INTER-
VIEWED IN PARIS YESTERDAY, HE STATED THAT HE
WAS QUITE CONVINCED BY THIS TIME THAT MISS
ASHE HAS BEEN KIDNAPPED IN ORDER TO EXTORT
A RANSOM AND HE WAS EXPECTING ANY DAY TO
HEAR FROM THOSE WHO HAD ABDUCTED HER.

HE HAS REITERATED THAT HIS WIFE AND HE
HAVE SUCH A DEEP AFFECTION FOR MISS ASHE
THAT THEY FONDLY HOPE SHE MAY IN TIME BE-
COME THEIR DAUGHTER-IN-LAW.

Reading what was printed in the newspapers, Lord Kirkly thought the *Comte* was being very clever in staking his claim on Otila.

It would mean when she was found that every sort of pressure would be put upon her to marry one of the Chalon sons.

It struck him that it was almost like seeing her

drawn by the tentacles of an octopus deeper and deeper into its embrace so that it would be almost impossible for her to disentangle herself and when finally she was discovered, to assert her independence.

"I have to save her," he told himself.

He felt that what he had said to her when she was delirious was almost in the nature of a vow and a promise he should not break.

He also realised that his idea of sending her away from him was no longer the answer to the problem, as he had previously thought it would be.

He was well aware that he was under an obligation that he could not ignore.

He did not underestimate the damage which the Ambassador, inflamed with jealousy in an uncontrolled rage, would have inflicted upon him, but for Otila's intervention.

If she was suffering from one thrust of the foil, he could imagine what his plight would have been if, as the Ambassador intended, he had mutilated both his arms and perhaps even his face.

"No other woman I have ever met," Lord Kirkly told himself as he walked between bushes of bougainvillaea, "would have been so brave and so resourceful!"

When he came to consider it, he could not think of one woman of his acquaintance who knew anything about fencing or would have had the slightest idea what to do, even if she held a foil in her hand.

Otila's intervention had been brilliant.

It had given him time to rise from the armchair, seize a foil from the wall, and defeat the Ambassador in a manner that left him defenceless and humiliated.

"Otila saved me!" Lord Kirkly said to himself not once but a dozen times as he walked through the garden.

He knew that in return he had to save her.

He heard somebody call him and looked up to see Bates waving to him from the balcony of Otila's Bedroom.

He knew this meant that she was waiting to see him, and there was a smile on his face as he walked into the cool marble-floored Hall, with its Greek pillars, and up to the beautifully carved marble staircase which led to the first floor.

Bates was waiting for him at the door of Otila's room, and when he reached it he said:

"Miss Otila's 'er old self again this morning, M'Lord. Happy as a sand-boy, an' I thinks she'll be well enough to be up on her feet in a day or two."

"I hope you are right, Bates," Lord Kirkly said as he walked into the Bedroom.

Otila was propped up against a number of lace-trimmed pillows, her hair brushed until it seemed to have caught the rays of the sun, and tied neatly with a bow of blue ribbon, which made her look like a schoolgirl.

She held out her hands to him, saying:

"I am so excited to be here, but I cannot remember how I arrived, unless you carried me on a magic carpet!"

"Actually, you were asleep," Lord Kirkly said, "but I think you will find there are a lot of magical things here to amuse you, and Bates expects you to be well enough to come exploring with me in two days time!"

"That will be wonderful!" Otila cried. "I would love to go exploring. It is what I have always wanted to do . . . with you."

As she spoke she suddenly knew she was virtually pushing herself upon him and insinuating that she wished to come with him to Tunis, and the colour rose faintly to her cheeks.

She looked away from him towards the open window, and Lord Kirkly sat down on the side of the bed.

"I have been walking in the garden," he said, "trying to think how I can reward you for what you did for me."

"I do not . . . want you to . . . do that," Otila said. "My reward . . . is simply that I am still with you . . . and you have not yet sent me away . . . alone."

There was a little tremor in her voice before the last word and Lord Kirkly knew that was what was frightening her.

"We are not going to talk about that," he said. "I wonder if, amongst your other talents, you have ever learnt to play chess?"

"Of course I have!" Otila replied. "It was one of Papa's favourite games in the winter."

"Good! I noticed last night when I dined alone that my grandmother has a magnificent chessboard made of onyx and crystal, with the chessmen all carved in precious stones."

Otila clasped her hands together.

"Will you play with me?"

"That is what I have every intention of doing,"

Lord Kirkly replied, "and I will tell Bates to fetch the board."

* * *

Later that night, when Otila was told she must sleep in order to get well quickly, she thought the day she had spent alone with Lord Kirkly had been one of the happiest in her life.

He had not talked of the difficulties there would be in the future, and he had not told her what was in the newspapers.

But between games of chess he had brought to her bedside some of the smaller objects which his grandmother had collected over the years and which were very beautiful.

She had written little accounts of each one of them—where she had found it and what its history was.

Lord Kirkly realised it had given him an interest he had never had before to explain to Otila the background of the Grecian and Roman carvings on which he was in fact an acknowledged expert.

It was something, however, that he seldom talked about, because the men with whom he spent his time in England were too interested in sport to think about what they referred to as his "idiosyncracies."

The women whom he found attractive and who found him irresistible were interested only in the present insofar as it included them, and had no wish to delve into the past.

To Otila, however, everything he told her was a delight, and he knew her interest was completely genuine, with nothing forced or pretentious about it.

"Tell me more . . . tell me more!" she kept saying, until laughingly he had to tell her that he would have to do a great deal more research before he could oblige her.

"He is so clever!" Otila murmured against her pillow. "How could anyone ever be bored if they were with him?"

Then she told herself humbly that she could never hope that he would say the same about her.

It was now she really admitted to herself what she had learnt after being injured by the Ambassador— that she loved Lord Kirkly.

It seemed incredible, after thinking that she hated all men so violently, to know that she loved him and to feel sure she was not mistaken by the feeling he evoked in her every time he came near her, in fact, every time she thought about him.

He made her feel so different from anything she had ever felt in her life before: like the sudden leap of her heart whenever he came into a room.

There was an irresistible sensation in her breast which made it difficult to speak naturally, and when he touched her hand she felt as if little sparks of light ran from it until her body thrilled and thrilled again.

"I love him!" she said to herself.

Then she despairingly knew that, whilst she had changed her views in a manner she had never expected to, he was not interested in her as a woman.

"He is kind to me because I am so helpless," Otila told herself, "and now he feels he is under obligation because I saved him from the Ambassador."

But she knew that what she wanted was something different.

She wanted Lord Kirkly to love her because she was a woman, to want her as she wanted him.

She was not at all certain exactly what that meant. She only knew what she felt when he was there, and that, if he held her in his arms, it would be like being in Heaven.

"I love him! I love him!"

She repeated the words over and over again.

Then somehow, because it was so hopeless and she knew even to think of him loving her was like looking at the moon and wishing one could touch it, she felt the tears spring into her eyes.

She knew that was why she was crying, but at the same time it was something much deeper than that.

She was crying because the tears came from her heart, a heart that was throbbing and yearning for a man to whom she was nothing more than a tiresome child who had imposed herself upon him.

"I love him!" she said again and again, until from sheer exhaustion she fell asleep.

* * *

The following day Otila was well enough to be lifted onto the balcony to have luncheon there with Lord Kirkly.

The food was delicious and the old cook, who had been there in his grandmother's time, was determined to make a feast of every meal.

There was also a golden wine, which had been kept

in the cellars for exactly the right amount of time, and was cooled by Bates until it was to Lord Kirkly's liking.

When the meal was over he said to Otila:

"Now you must rest for at least two hours."

"I want to be with you," she said quickly.

He shook his head.

"You are still under the Doctor's orders, or rather mine, and I know that every invalid has to have a *siesta* after luncheon, as do all good Italians if they get the chance. So go to sleep, Otila, and when you wake up I will bring you some more of my grandmother's treasures, and we will have a competition as to who can tell the best story about them."

"Which you will win!" Otila cried. "You know so much more than I do. I was thinking last night before I went to sleep how clever you are."

"Now you are flattering me!" Lord Kirkly said. "I think you will find, as I do, that the more one learns, the more there is to know."

Otila laughed, and it was a very happy sound.

"I shall try to beat you," she said, "so I will go to sleep just so that my brain will be quick and fresh and ready to deal with you!"

She paused before she said:

"One day . . . will you give me a . . . fencing lesson? It is what I would enjoy more than anything else!"

"That is something I never expected a woman to ask of me," Lord Kirkly said, "but of course I will and when it is safe we will go back to Antonio Caruso's School and he and I will give you the exhibition I promised you before we were so rudely interrupted!"

Otila's eyes lit up, and he knew before she spoke that what she was really thinking was that if he had promised her that, it meant he was not yet ready to leave for Tunis and send her away alone.

As Bates lowered the curtains and shut the sun blinds so that Otila could sleep, Lord Kirkly went downstairs and was just deliberating whether he would sit in the garden or in one of the attractive rooms inside the Villa, when he saw a carriage turn in at the gates and come up the short drive that led to the front door.

Lord Kirkly looked at it in surprise, wondering who could be calling on him.

Then as he stood in the hall he saw through the open door Jules de Chalon step out of the carriage.

He looked, Lord Kirkly thought scornfully, rather more over-dressed than when he had last seen him at the Railway Station, and he thought his "ferrety" looks, as if his search for Otila had made him become un-pleasantly inquisitive.

As Jules de Chalon walked towards the front door, which was open, he saw Lord Kirkly, and it was too late for the latter to move away and say he was not receiving callers.

Instead, remembering he was not supposed to know who this gentleman was, he stood looking aloof and somewhat disdainful, as if he had no wish to have his privacy interrupted.

Jules de Chalon bowed and said:

"I think you are Lord Kirkly!"

"I am."

"I am Jules de Chalon, and I should be most grateful, My Lord, if I might have a few words with you in private."

Lord Kirkly thought it would be wise to be reasonably affable and replied:

"Of course, but I am a little pressed for time."

"This will not take long," Jules de Chalon said.

Lord Kirkly led the way into the Library, which was an attractive room with bookcases built into two walls, while the other walls were hung with extremely beautiful pictures which his grandmother had collected arduously during the years she had lived in Italy.

There was a great bowl of flowers on one table, and flowers filled the fireplace that was not in use during the summer.

Lord Kirkly indicated an armchair and sat down in one opposite, which had a high back and gave him an almost regal look.

"I understand you arrived in Italy four days ago from France," Jules de Chalon began.

"That is correct," Lord Kirkly agreed.

The way he answered made it quite obvious that he thought it was none of de Chalon's business and he was in fact surprised at being questioned.

"I think we must have travelled here on the same train," Jules de Chalon went on, "and now that I see you I remember noticing you on the platform."

"I cannot imagine why my movements should be of any particular interst to you, *Monsieur*," Lord Kirkly said.

"You were with a lady in a wheel-chair"—Jules de Chalon went on as if he had not been interrupted—

"and I should be interested to know, My Lord, exactly who that lady was!"

Lord Kirkly raised his eyebrows as if affronted by the Frenchman's impertinence, and sat up a little straighter in his chair.

"I fail to understand what my movements as an individual should have to do with you," he said, "or why you have come here uninvited to ask me questions about my private life!"

"I expect you have seen the reports in the newspaper about a missing heiress," Jules de Chalon said.

Lord Kirkly appeared to be pondering the question for a moment before he replied.

"I believe I did see a mention of it."

"I am investigating the disappearance of this young lady, who had been staying in Paris with my family," Jules de Chalon explained. "She is very wealthy and we therefore suspect she has been kidnapped in order to extort a ransom."

"I cannot believe you are insinuating that I am a kidnapper!" Lord Kirkly said sharply.

"Or," Jules de Chalon went on as if Lord Kirkly had not spoken, "she may have been assisted to escape by some English friend."

"I do not quite understand," Lord Kirkly said. "Escape? From what—and from whom?"

It was a question that was obviously unexpected, and for a moment Jules de Chalon hesitated. Then he said:

"Young girls sometimes have strange ideas in their heads, and there is a chance—just a chance—that Otila Ashe ran away because she wished to feel free of constraint and, of course, the chaperonage which is compulsory where every young woman is concerned."

"If that is what she did—good luck to her!" Lord Kirkly said.

He rose to his feet.

"I am afraid it is impossible for me to give you any more of my time, *Monsieur*. I can only hope you succeed in finding this young lady, which I cannot believe is a very difficult task."

"It is difficult unless people are honest with us and tell us the truth."

Although Lord Kirkly was standing, Jules de Chalon had not moved and he went on.

"You have not answered my question, My Lord, as to who was the lady, or girl, you escorted from the train in a wheel-chair."

Lord Kirkly drew himself to his full height and dignity.

"I consider your curiosity, *Monsieur*, extremely impertinent and an intrusion into my private affairs. But I have nothing to hide, and therefore prepared to answer that the lady who has aroused your interest is, in fact, my wife. However, I see no reason why you or anybody else should cross-question me as regards a missing person in whom I have no interest whatsoever. May I suggest therefore that you look elsewhere! I regret I have no further time to waste. Good-day!"

There was nothing Jules de Chalon could do but rise slowly to his feet.

"I can only apologise, My Lord, for having bothered you," he said, "but my father and my brothers, and, of course, myself are desperately concerned as to what has happened to Miss Otila Ashe."

"You have all my sympathy," Lord Kirkly said curtly. "At the same time, as I am a busy man, you must excuse me."

He opened the door of the room, holding it so that Jules de Chalon was obliged to leave.

He walked with an air of contrived jauntiness across the Hall and down the steps to where his carriage was waiting.

A footman opened the door for him, then climbed onto the box and the horses moved off.

Lord Kirkly watched him go and only when the carriage was out of sight and had turned out of the Villa gates did he give a deep sigh.

As he did so Bates came from the shadows at the far end of the Hall.

"That's the man we saw on the station, M'Lord!" he said.

"Yes, I know," Lord Kirkly agreed.

"Do you think he believed you could tell him nothin'?"

"I think so," Lord Kirkly said, "but I cannot be certain, and it is difficult, Bates, to know what to do next."

"Well, we can't have Miss Otila upset—that's for certain!" Bates said quickly.

"No, of course not," Lord Kirkly agreed. "She must not know that Jules de Chalon has been here, and we must make certain that nobody in the house tells her of his visit."

"I'll make sure o' that, M'Lord, but if you asks me, that 'Frenchy' is suspicious all right. He's like a dog with 'is nose to the ground, scenting his prey, an' he won't give up until he finds her."

Lord Kirkly did not reply. He merely walked away from Bates, down the steps that led into the garden.

Then as he walked amongst the flowers with the sunshine dazzling his eyes he knew what he must do.

chapter seven

OTILA awoke from a deep sleep and realised she had been dreaming of Lord Kirkly.

In her dream he had been carrying her in his arms and she had felt safe and no longer afraid of anything.

When she woke she lay for some time with her eyes closed, imagining that his arms were still around her, her cheek against his shoulder.

Because it was such a lovely dream she had no wish to wake up completely until she remembered he was here in the Villa and she could see him. She was so afraid of losing him that she did not want to miss a moment of being with him in reality.

"I love him!" she told herself for the millionth time.

"How can I ever manage without him?"

She felt a little shiver of fear go through her at the thought of how terrifying it would be when she was alone and still being pursued by the Chalons.

It made her open her eyes.

The beautiful white Bedroom was touched with gold from the sun seeping through the blinds over the windows, and she longed to go back to sleep again and into her dream of being close to Lord Kirkly.

Then as she wondered whether she should ring for the chambermaids to come and tidy her, there was a knock on the door, and when she did not answer, Bates opened it very quietly and peeped inside.

"Are you awake, Miss?" he asked needlessly when he saw her looking at him.

"I am awake," Otila replied.

"You've had a nice long sleep, and that's good!" Bates said in the tone of an approving Nanny.

He opened the door wider and carried in a huge vase of Madonna lilies which he set down beside Otila.

"How lovely!" she exclaimed. "I adore lilies!"

"There's masses of 'em in the garden," Bates replied, "and p'raps tomorrow you'll be able to get up and see them."

"That is what I intend to do," Otila said. "I am tired of staying in bed."

Bates did not answer, but went back to the door to bring in another vase of lilies which he set down on the other side of the bed.

With the background of the white muslin curtains, it made Otila feel she was a Fairy Princess in a bower of flowers.

Sitting up against the pillows, she asked:

"What time is it?"

"Nearly half past four, Miss," Bates replied.

Otila gave a little cry of surprise.

"I have slept for hours! No wonder I feel so well!"

"'Is Lordship's waitin' to see you."

"Tell him I will be ready in five minutes," Otila replied.

As she spoke, the Italian maids came in, bringing her a fresh nightgown, which was even prettier than the one she had on.

She had been very extravagant in buying the most beautiful and elaborate *lingerie* obtainable in the whole of Paris.

When she was wearing the nightgown of diaphanous material trimmed with real lace, with a chiffon scarf also trimmed with lace to wear over it, she thought secretly that it was more attractive than any Ballgown.

The maids brushed her hair until the red lights in it seemed to dance in the sunshine, and they caught it up on either side of her forehead with two small diamond stars which she told them to bring her from her jewel-case.

The whole room looked beautiful now, and the lilies added to its loveliness. She knew she wanted to create a picture that Lord Kirkly would remember when they parted.

She was sure, however, that he would not be alone with his thoughts and memories for long.

There would be some lovely lady to amuse him, and because Otila had seen in Paris the elegance of both the *Monde* and the *Demi-Monde* as they drove about the Bois or shopped in the Rue de la Paix, she thought it was impossible for her to compare with them, and she could understand that Lord Kirkly found her nothing but a bore.

This did not prevent her, however, from watching the door excitedly when the maids and Bates had left her alone in her Bedroom.

They had raised the sun-blinds, and now she could see outside the window the palm-trees moving just slightly in the breeze from the sea, while beyond them was the vivid blue of the Mediterranean.

It flashed through Otila's mind that it was a perfect setting for love, and she wondered what she would feel if she were here with somebody whom she loved as much as she loved Lord Kirkly, and who loved her.

Then she told herself miserably that no man could ever love her for herself, and even if they did, she would always be suspicious that it was her money that enticed them.

Because the thought of the love she could never have and which would always remain out of reach made her feel miserable, she felt the tears come into her eyes.

Then the door opened and they were swept away, as with the familiar leap of her heart she realised that Lord Kirkly had come into the room.

"Bates told me you were ready for me," he said as he walked towards her.

She thought he seemed to come to her in a blaze of light, and it was hard to answer him coherently.

He reached the bed and stood looking down at her.

As her eyes met his questioningly he said:

"You look very lovely, and I think these will complete the picture."

As he spoke he put into her hands a bunch of white orchids.

As she took them from him her fingers touched his, and she felt herself thrill.

"Thank ... you," she said with a little tremor in her voice.

To her surprise Lord Kirkly sat down on the bed facing her and took her hand in his.

"I have brought you the orchids, Otila," he said, "for a special reason."

Because he was touching her, it was hard to concentrate on what he was saying.

She realised he was speaking in a quiet, serious voice, and she thought there was a strange expression in his eyes that she had not seen before.

"Early this afternoon," Lord Kirkly said, "Jules de Chalon called here."

Otila gave a little exclamation of horror, and her fingers tightened frantically on his.

"And this evening," he went on, "the Chief of Police for Naples has intimated that he wishes to see me."

Now a cry came from Otila from the very depths of her heart as she said frantically:

"They are suspicious. They have ... guessed I am here. I ... must go away ... I must hide ... help me please ... help me!"

As she spoke she looked round the room desperately, as if she thought the walls would open to show her some magic place where she could become invisible.

"I agree with you," Lord Kirkly said quietly, "that they are suspicious, and I should imagine if the Police make enquiries, which they undoubtedly will, they will be aware that up to now I have been an unmarried man."

"If they . . . really suspect," Otila said in a small voice, "you will be in . . . trouble for having . . . altered your passport."

"You are thinking of me?"

"Of course I am thinking of . . . you," Otila replied. "I would not wish you to be . . . involved in any . . . scandal. I must go away! Tell me . . . please, tell me where . . . I can . . . go."

"I have a far better idea than that," Lord Kirkly answered, "but I am afraid to tell you about it in case it frightens you."

"The only thing that . . . frightens me is having to leave you . . . knowing the Chalons will be . . . waiting ready to . . . get me back into . . . their clutches."

There was a note of terror in her voice which Lord Kirkly did not miss, and after a moment he asked:

"Would you prefer to stay with me?"

"Of course I . . . want to . . . stay with you!" Otila cried. "It is only with you that I feel safe . . . but that is . . . impossible . . . so I have to . . . go away."

Her voice broke on the last words, and she looked up at Lord Kirkly as if she were seeing him for the last time and memorising every feature of his face so that she could never forget it.

"There is one means by which you can really be safe, Otila," Lord Kirkly said slowly, "one by which you would never need to feel afraid again."

"What is . . . that?" Otila asked hopefully. "And why have you not . . . told me of it . . . before?"

Unexpectedly Lord Kirkly smiled.

"I wanted to," he said, "but you have been so positive that you hated men that I was afraid, in view of the fact that I am a man, of suggesting such a solution that would involve me!"

"But you are . . . different!" Otila said. "So very . . . very . . . different! When I said I hated men I did not . . . mean . . . you. Actually—"

She stopped suddenly as if she felt that what she was about to say would be too revealing. Her eyelashes flickered as she looked away from him and the colour rose in her cheeks.

"I want to hear you complete that sentence," Lord Kirkly said.

"No . . . no!" Otila said quickly. "Tell me . . . how I can be safe . . . that is what I . . . want to hear."

"It is quite simple: You will be safe, completely and absolutely safe, Otila, if you stay with me!"

She looked again at him, her eyes puzzled and questioning.

"I—I do not . . . understand . . . the Police are already suspicious that I am not . . . what I am pretending to be."

"What I am suggesting," Lord Kirkly said, "is that we simply eliminate the pretence. In fact, Otila, I have arranged for our marriage to take place—now— immediately, in fact!"

He still spoke in the same quiet, deep voice he had used since coming into her room, but as Otila felt she could not have heard him right, she just stared at him.

Her eyes grew wider and wider until they seemed to fill her whole face.

Then she said, and her voice seemed to come from far away:

"Wh-what are you saying . . . to me? What are you telling . . . me?"

"I am telling you, my darling, that the only way I can protect you properly as I want to, the only way I can make sure that you will not be dragged away from me or kidnapped for your money, is to make you truly my wife!"

Otila's eyes seemed to be filled with the light of a thousand candles.

Then as her fingers tightened on Lord Kirkly's she said:

"Are you really . . . saying that you . . . will marry me?"

"It is all arranged," he replied. "The Parson is here waiting, and once I have put the ring on your finger, there will be no more difficulties, no more fears, and I think we will be very happy together."

"I—I cannot believe it! I think I am . . . dreaming!"

Lord Kirkly smiled. Then he said:

"It will be a rather strange wedding, very different, I am sure, from anything you can ever have expected. I must explain to you that in order to avoid being involved in all the Italian formalities, which would inevitably attract the Press, we are going to be married according to the Church of Scotland."

Otila was still staring at him, and her face was so radiant that he thought it would be impossible for any woman to look lovelier.

As if he knew that she must understand, he went on.

"I have therefore arranged for a Presbyterian Minister, who is the head here of the British Mission to Seaman, to marry us according to Scottish Law, which is more simple as regards marriage than British, but, I must add, just as binding."

"And . . . I will really be your . . . wife?"

"There is no doubt about that," Lord Kirkly assured her. "As it happens, and that is something you will learn more of later, my mother was a MacDonald, so when I asked the Minister, whose name is Fergus McTavish, to perform our marriage ceremony, it was Scot speaking to Scot, and there were no difficulties."

As he finished speaking Lord Kirkly rose from the bed and as he was still holding Otila's hand in his, he kissed it before he laid it down gently on the sheet beside her bouquet.

Then he walked across the room to the door, and a second later the Reverend Fergus McTavish came into the room.

It was a very short ceremony but performed movingly by a man whose sincerity came from the very depths of his Scottish heart.

First Lord Kirkly then Otila repeated after the Minister the words which made them man and wife.

It was very quiet in the Bedroom, with only the buzz of the bees outside in the garden, but it seemed to Otila that there was the soft music of angel voices and the flutter of their wings overhead as the Minister said:

"Those whom God hath joined together let no man put asunder!"

She could hardly believe it was true, and yet as

she felt Lord Kirkly putting a ring on her finger she knew that her prayers had been answered and she was safe—safe for all time as the wife of the man she loved.

Only a short while ago she had thought that he was as far out of reach as the moon, and the future was dark and terrifying because she had lost him.

Yet now he was tying her to him by vows that were so sacred that she knew that neither of them would ever break them, and his ring, which denoted Eternity, encircled her finger and made her his.

"I love you! I love you!" she wanted to cry aloud.

As the Minister blessed them, she felt as if the love that came from God Himself enveloped them both in an aura of glory.

Then she heard her own voice as if it came from another world thanking the Minister and saying good-bye, and Lord Kirkly accompanied him through the door of the Bedroom.

For a moment Otila was alone, and she could only ask herself wildly if what was happening was really true and not part of a dream from which she would suddenly awake to find herself even more frightened than before.

Then Lord Kirkly came back, shutting the door behind him, and she could only stare at him, holding her bouquet as if for support.

He looked happier than she had ever seen him.

The lines of cynicism seemed to have gone from his face, and he was smiling as he said:

"Now the formalities are over, may I take off my coat and be comfortable?"

He did not wait for her reply but took off his coat

150

and threw it down on a chair as he sat upon the bed facing her as he had done before, except that this time he seemed a little nearer.

Their eyes met and she asked a little incoherently:

"Is . . . is it . . . true? Is it . . . really true that we are married?"

"We are married, Otila, and you are my wife!"

"B-but you did not . . . wish to be married . . . and you . . . h-hated women . . . as I . . . hated men!"

"That was before I knew you," Lord Kirkly said, "and I think we both said a lot of foolish things which neither of us really meant."

"I—I did hate men . . . except you."

"And now what do you feel about me?"

Because his face seemed very near to hers, she suddenly felt shy and found it difficult to answer him.

"I want to know the truth, Otila," he said. "It is very important indeed for me to know it!"

"It is . . . difficult to tell you what . . . I feel."

"Why?"

"Because it is . . . something you . . . may not . . . want to . . . hear."

"I want to hear what you feel about me more than I want anything else at the moment," Lord Kirkly said, "and it is very unlike you, Otila, to be coy."

As this was not what she expected him to say, she said defensively:

"I—I am not . . . coy—"

"Then you are shy," he interrupted, "and that I find very intriguing, and also exciting."

She gave him a quick glance, then looked away again.

Because he was so near to her she could feel her

heart beating frantically and there were little thrills running through her body.

"I am waiting for a reply to my first question," he said gently. "What do you feel about me? I think and hope I know the answer, but I want to hear you say it."

Now he was nearer than ever and the words seemed to burst from her as if she could no longer control them.

"I love . . . you! I love . . . you! But I cannot . . . believe that you . . . love me!"

"Then I shall have to convince you that I do," he said, and his lips were on hers.

For a moment Otila could not breathe.

Then as she felt her whole being respond to his kiss, she knew this was love as she had always sought it, a love so overwhelming, so violent, that she had no defence against it.

Lord Kirkly's arms tightened around her and his lips became more insistent, more demanding.

To Otila it was everything she had longed for, dreamt of, but thought that because of her money it would never be hers.

She could feel the vibrations coming from him as she had felt them before, only now so strong, so demanding, that they held her captive.

She knew that there was no escape from a love that was compelling and to which she could only surrender herself completely.

Lord Kirkly kissed her until she gave him not only her heart, but also her soul.

Then as she could feel his hand through the thin

material of her nightgown, and she felt sensations she did not even know existed, she knew that Lord Kirkly was no longer out of reach like the moon.

She was a part of him and as she gave him her body, they were not two people but one.

* * *

A long time later, when the sun was sinking in all its glory and the sky was darkening overhead, Otila turned her face against her husband's shoulder and whispered:

"Do you . . . still love me?"

Lord Kirkly's arms tightened as he said:

"I did not know it was possible to love anyone so much or find a woman who was so perfect, Otila!"

"Do you really . . . mean that?"

"I do mean it, my precious," he replied, "but I have not hurt or frightened you?"

"You took me up into Heaven, where there is no fear, and I know now I shall never be . . . frightened again."

"That is what I wanted you to say and I think, my darling, you realise that I am not a fortune-hunter and not at all interested in your money!"

Otila laughed. It was a very happy, spontaneous laugh, and she said:

"For the first time since my grandfather died I had forgotten about my millions of dollars."

"It is something you need never think about in the future," Lord Kirkly said, "because I have already decided that we will set up a trust to help people wherever it is needed, and the money you will spend, my precious, will be my money, and about that there will be no argument!"

There was silence until suddenly Lord Kirkly asked:

"You are not crying, my precious? What have I said to make you cry?"

Otila hid her face against him and he could feel her tears on his shoulder.

"It is . . . because I am so . . . happy," she sobbed. "I thought no one would ever . . . love me for . . . myself."

"I was foolish to think the same for myself," Lord Kirkly said, "until I knew I loved you so overwhelmingly that I would have married you even if the whole world had tried to stop me or drove me into exile!"

"Do . . . you mean . . . that?"

"I mean it and a great deal more! I have married you, darling, because I love you as you are and I adore my wife, whatever she has or has not."

He pulled her a little closer and ran his hand gently over her body before he said:

"Actually I prefer you with nothing, as you are at the moment."

Otila made a little sound which was half a sob and half a laugh before she said:

"How can you be so wonderful as to frighten away all the bogeys which have been haunting me and making me so miserable? And how could I have been so clever as to know when you came into the Hotel Meurice that you were the only man in the world who could make me happy?"

Lord Kirkly's arms tightened around her. Then he said:

"I wonder if anyone has found your dress-boxes yet?"

Otila pressed herself a little closer to him.

"Supposing you had sent me away," she said, "as you wanted to do? By now I would be back in the clutches of the Chalons, and doubtless be married to Jules!"

"You are not to think about it!" Lord Kirkly said sharply. "And if that conceited young Frenchman comes anywhere near you, I will smash him in the face, which is what I longed to do this afternoon when he came asking me a lot of impertinent questions!"

Otila held on to Lord Kirkly as if she was again afraid she might lose him. Then she said:

"He . . . cannot touch . . . me now!"

"No one can touch you, no one can frighten you," he said. "You are mine, Otila, and I will not have you upset."

She gave a sigh of relief.

Then as if she could not express herself in any other way she kissed his naked shoulder again, saying as she did so:

"I love . . . you! I love . . . you! You are the most wonderful . . . man in the whole . . . world!"

"That is what I want you to think."

He put his fingers under her chin and turned her face up to his.

"I suppose you know how much you have tortured me," he said, "because I was afraid you really meant it when you said you hated all men and would never marry."

"And I was tortured when I realised I loved you," Otila replied, "and thought you found me only a . . .

155

nuisance and a . . . bore!"

"You could never, never be that!"

Before she could protest further, he was kissing her again, kissing her fervently, insistently, until the flames of love rose again within them.

As they drew closer and closer, Otila could hear once again the angels singing, and knew that Lord Kirkly was lifting her into their special Heaven where there was only sunshine and love.

*   *   *

The Chief of Police in Naples had waited for nearly an hour before Lord Kirkly came to join him in the Sitting-Room of the Villa.

He might have been annoyed had not Bates kept him supplied not only with an excellent wine, which was far superior to anything he was used to drinking, but also with delicious sweetmeats.

These were made with almonds and honey and were, as it happened, one of the Chief of Police's favourite dishes.

When Lord Kirkly finally came into the room, the Chief quickly wiped his sticky fingers before taking His Lordship's outstretched hand.

"I can only apologise most sincerely for keeping you waiting," Lord Kirkly said, "but it was in fact unavoidable."

As he spoke, Bates brought in a fresh bottle of wine and Lord Kirkly said:

"I am going to ask you a very great favour, Chief."

The Italian looked surprised before he said:

"I have come here to ask you some rather embarrassing questions, My Lord, which arise from information we have received from a reliable source which cannot be ignored."

Lord Kirkly smiled and said:

"I can guess what those questions are. You think I am hiding here in my Villa the lost heiress who disappeared and is being searched for by the French and Italian Police. Is that not correct?"

"Quite correct, My Lord, but you will appreciate I have no wish to offend Your Lordship by my enquiries, which nevertheless have to be made."

"I understand that," Lord Kirkly agreed. "I therefore have a proposition to put to you first and I hope you will agree."

As he spoke, the Chief of Police looked slightly apprehensive but he went on.

"I am prepared to answer your questions truthfully and fully on one condition. But before you say that it might be difficult for you to agree, let me beg of you, not as a Policeman but as a man who I am sure understands love, to be sympathetic."

The way Lord Kirkly spoke made, as he expected, the Chief of Police look not only intrigued but also flattered and he continued.

"What I am asking is quite simple; that the information I give you, and which will be known to no one else, will be kept a secret until my wife and I have left the country."

He paused, then he said:

"That will be tomorrow night, or the following day, and we are leaving on a yacht that is at the moment in Naples harbour and which I have managed to charter for the next two months. It belongs to the Duke of Oporto, and I have been able to lease it through the good offices of my friend Antonio Caruso."

The Chief of Police was obviously impressed and he said:

"I know the yacht in question, My Lord. It is a very fine vessel. The Duke has expended a great deal of money on it."

"It is exactly what I needed for my honeymoon."

Lord Kirkly saw the Chief of Police raise his eyebrows at the word. Then he smiled, and picking up his glass said:

"I want you, Chief, to drink to my happiness, and I assure you, I feel as if I am at this moment the happiest and luckiest man in the whole world!"

"You are really married, *Signor?*" the Chief of Police asked. "I understood from the enquiries I have made that there is no record of your marriage."

"In fact I am married," Lord Kirkly said, "and I have my marriage certificate to show you. But I am asking you to collaborate with me just until the day after tomorrow, so that my wife, who has not been well and would find the attention of the Press very unwelcome and extremely intrusive, can leave Naples incognito."

The Chief of Police took a deep breath as if he needed it. Then he asked:

"Are you telling me, My Lord, that you have married this heiress, Miss Otila Ashe?"

Lord Kirkly smiled.

"I thought you would be quick-witted enough to

guess that is the truth! You will realise that the last thing we want at the moment is to be tracked down and have dozens of journalists asking us a lot of questions we should both find very embarrassing."

His eyes twinkled as he went on.

"I am sure you, as a man of the world, will know that love, especially for a young girl, is something so personal, so intimate, that one wants to keep it to one's self."

There was no need for words, for Lord Kirkly could see the sympathetic expression on the face of the Chief of Police, and he went on.

"You and you alone, Chief, will be able to break the news to the world, which has given far too much attention to Miss Ashe and her fortune, of what has actually happened. I assure you that in future I shall protect her very carefully from the attentions of the journalists who, in my opinion, ask too many impertinent questions, even though it is their job to do so."

"I understand, My Lord," the Chief of Police said. "I understand completely what you are feeling."

"Then you will help us?"

He knew the answer before the Chief of Police took his outstretched hand and proceeded to drink both his and Otila's health several times before he was ready to depart.

"All you have to do, in order to make sure there is no mistake," Lord Kirkly said, "is to assure your colleagues that you are hot on the trail and are making searching enquiries to which you are confident of having an answer by the day after tomorrow."

He gave a laugh before he added:

"I am so glad, Chief, that it will be your picture that will decorate the front page of every newspaper in this country as well as in France, and of course, England, rather than my own!"

In front of his very eyes the Chief of Police seemed to swell with his own importance before he replied:

"Everything will be exactly as you suggest, My Lord."

"And to show my gratitude," Lord Kirkly went on, "I hope you will accept a contribution from my wife and myself towards the Police Benevolent Fund in Naples. I have already made out the cheque, but as I am not certain what the proper name of your department is, I have left that for you to fill in."

The Chief of Police hastily put the envelope in which the cheque was enclosed into the inside pocket of his tunic.

Then once again he was offering Lord Kirkly his good wishes for his future happiness and of course that of his wife, and that their union would be blessed with an abundance of sons.

Only when Lord Kirkly had seen him drive away and waved him good-bye did he run hastily up the stairs to Otila's Bedroom.

As he entered the room she held out her arms, saying as she did so:

"Was it all right? Oh, darling, I was praying it would be all right!"

"Everything went just as I had planned!" Lord Kirkly said. "He was very thrilled at the idea that he and he alone will solve the mystery of the missing heiress, and he has promised us Police protection and will see that we board the yacht unmolested early the day after tomorrow."

"Board a yacht?" Otila asked.

"Did I forget to tell you?" Lord Kirkly asked. "It is not surprising, my precious, when I find it hard to think of anything but you."

He kissed her as he spoke, and as she put her arms around his neck and drew him closer to her, it was impossible to think of anything but the excited beat of their hearts and the little flames of fire rising within them both.

Then Otila said in a slightly unsteady voice:

"T-tell me about . . . the yacht . . . my darling . . . wonderful husband . . . otherwise . . . if you . . . kiss me again . . . I shall forget everything . . . except how much I love you!"

"That is all I really want you to remember," Lord Kirkly said. "In fact, I hired the yacht, which was something I arranged while you were asleep, yesterday after luncheon through Antonio Caruso."

"And we shall have it all to ourselves?"

"Except for a number of seamen, we shall be quite alone," he said with a smile.

"It sounds . . . too wonderful! You know I want to be alone with you . . . so that you . . . can teach me about . . . love."

"That is what I want to do," he said, "and it is going to take me a long time, my darling, and will require a great many lessons!"

"It will be very . . . very wonderful for me."

"And for me," Lord Kirkly replied, "and because you are so sweet, so different from any other woman

161

I have known, I think that I too will have a lot to learn, as well as to teach."

Otila laughed, and it was a very attractive sound.

"That I cannot believe! You know how ignorant I am and I am only . . . afraid I may do . . . something wrong and you will . . . no longer love me."

"That would be impossible!" Lord Kirkly assured her. "Everything you do is so perfect, so adorable, and, my precious, so madly exciting, that I know now I have never been in love before, and never, and this is the truth, been so happy."

Otila gave a cry of delight.

Then she was drawing him closer and still closer to her until she felt his hands touching her, his body close to hers.

She felt that their love was perfect, unique, and could never have happened to anyone else before.

It was a love that came from God, who had created them just for each other; a man and a woman who, joined by the Divine Power of Love, became one person, now and for all eternity.

ABOUT THE AUTHOR

Barbara Cartland, the world's most famous romantic novelist, who is also an historian, playwright, lecturer, political speaker and television personality, has now written over 400 books and sold over 390 million books the world over.

She has also had many historical works published and has written four autobiographies as well as the biographies of her mother and that of her brother, Ronald Cartland, who was the first Member of Parliament to be killed in the last war. This book has a preface by Sir Winston Churchill and has just been republished with an introduction by Sir Arthur Bryant.

Love at the Helm, a novel written with the help and inspiration of the late Admiral of the Fleet, the Earl Mountbatten of Burma, is being sold for the Mountbatten Memorial Trust.

Miss Cartland in 1978 sang an Album of Love Songs with the Royal Philharmonic Orchestra.

In 1976 by writing twenty-one books, she broke the world record and has continued for the following seven years with twenty-four, twenty, twenty-three, twenty-four, twenty-four, twenty-five, and twenty-three. She is in the *Guinness Book of Records* as the best-selling author in the world.

She is unique in that she was one and two in the Dalton List of Best Sellers, and one week had four books in the top twenty.

In private life Barbara Cartland, who is a Dame of the Order of St. John of Jerusalem, Chairman of the St. John Council in Hertfordshire and Deputy President of the St. John Ambulance Brigade, has also fought for better conditions and salaries for Midwives and Nurses.

Barbara Cartland is deeply interested in Vitamin Therapy and is President of the British National Association for Health. Her book *The Magic of Honey* has sold throughout the world and is translated into many languages. Her designs "Decorating with Love" are being sold all over the U.S.A., and the National Home Fashions League named her in 1981, "Woman of Achievement."

In 1984 she received at Kennedy Airport America's Bishop Wright Air Industry Award for her contribution to the development of aviation; in 1931 she and two R.A.F. Officers thought of, and carried, the first aeroplane-towed glider air-mail.

Barbara Cartland's Romances (a book of cartoons) has been published in Great Britain and the U.S.A., as well as a cookery book, *The Romance of Food*, and *Getting Older, Growing Younger*. She has recently written a children's pop-up picture book, entitled *Princess to the Rescue*.

BARBARA CARTLAND

Called after her own
beloved Camfield Place,
each Camfield novel of love
by Barbara Cartland
is a thrilling, never-before published
love story by the greatest romance
writer of all time.

April '86...HAUNTED
May '86...CROWNED WITH LOVE
June '86...ESCAPE
July '86...THE DEVIL DEFEATED